WHAT PEO̶P̶L̶E̶ ̶S̶A̶Y̶ ̶A̶BOUT DANIEL HE̶N̶S̶H̶A̶W̶...

"A GREAT PACEY READ.

PARENTS SHOULD READ THIS BOOK AS WELL AS KIDS. IT'S A LESSON LEARNT IN BEING HONEST, ALL WRAPPED UP IN A FUNNY STORY."

WRD ABOUT BOOKS MAGAZINE, *THE GREAT SNAIL ROBBERY*

"FULL OF HUMOUR AND TWISTS!"

STEWART FOSTER (AUTHOR OF THE BUBBLE BOY), *JEREMY'S SHORTS*

BOOKS BY DANIEL HENSHAW

THE GREAT SNAIL ROBBERY
THE CURIOUS CASE OF THE MISSING ORANGUTAN
JEREMY'S SHORTS
GLENKILLY

THE GREAT SNAIL ROBBERY

DANIEL HENSHAW

First published 2017

ISBN 9781521392089

Cover artwork and illustrations by Jimmy Rogers
booyeah.co.uk
Twitter: @jimmyrogers

For Fern

"I'm all of a sort."

CHAPTER ONE: DEATH OF A GOLDFISH

Our goldfish, Fanny, died on April 1st, three days after my tenth birthday.

I was eating burnt toast in the kitchen when Mum came in. She didn't look great. Her eyes were red, her hair was a mess and she was pulling that strange face she made when she was about to cry. She looked sadder than a turkey at Christmas. Either she had some bad news, or her hay fever was about to kick in.

"Jeremy," she said. "Fanny jumped out of your bedroom window and ended up in Mrs Patel's toolbox next door. She's dead now. Fanny, I mean. Not Mrs Patel."

I laughed at first, thinking it was an April Fool.

"Mum, you shouldn't joke about –"

Then I noticed she was actually crying and I realised that it wasn't an April Fool at all.

"Couldn't you save her?" I asked. "Did you try mouth-to-mouth?"

This sounded a lot more sensible in my head than when I said it out loud. I gave Mum a hug. It seemed a bit odd, a grown woman crying over a goldfish, but she'd been very emotional lately, with all the arguing she did with Dad.

Then I started crying too. My goldfish really was dead.

I'd always felt a bit sorry for Fanny. She must have been bored out of her mind in that empty tank. I mean, I get bored at school but at least I can look at the times-tables posters on the wall, which have funny aliens on them. Or sometimes, in the back of my book, I draw pictures of people with really long armpit hair.

What could Fanny do? Just swim around and around and around.

Still, I hadn't realised she was suicidal. So sad. Taking her dying breaths next to Mrs Patel's spanner. I'm not sure that's what Fanny would've wanted. The more I thought about it, the more I cried. And if I'd known how badly the death of a goldfish would later affect my family, I'd have somehow tried harder to save her.

2

Life didn't feel right without my goldfish.

A FAMILY ISN'T COMPLETE WITHOUT A PET!

I'd read that on a tea towel once.

*

Following Fanny's death, spending lunchtimes at school with Miss Hope cheered me up more than anything. Miss Hope was the kindest, most caring teacher in the school, probably in the world. She had a smile that could warm-up the frostiest morning. She was the most beautiful person I'd ever seen in real life (top secret information). She had long black hair and tanned skin like an Italian. She reminded me of Pocahontas from the Disney film.

Miss Hope let me stay in at lunchtimes because I helped to look after our class pets. Nobody else was interested in them. Just me.

"They disgucking," Leah Ford had said (she can't talk properly).

"They're dead boring," said Alfie Brown. "They're more boring than wallpaper… or radiators… or moss."

Everyone wanted hamsters or guinea pigs or even rats. Instead, we had two Giant African Land Snails... and I loved them!

Miss Hope had named them Pea and Pod because, when they were first born, they were smaller than her finger nail. Now they're bigger than both my hands put together. And I was the only person in class who dared pick them up. Even my best friend Michael didn't like touching them and his family are from Africa, just like the snails.

It was a Thursday lunchtime — just over a week since Fanny died — when Miss Hope said something that stuck in my brain like PVA glue.

Class was empty. Peaceful and quiet. Pod was greedily sucking on some cucumber, Pea was sliming his way across my hands and then Miss Hope gave me one of those smiles that made my heart skip.

"You must be filled with kindness, Jeremy," she said. "Because looking after animals fills your heart with kindness and love."

A tingle ran down my neck. *Miss Hope thought I was filled with kindness and love.* A warm glow surged through my body.

Miss Hope always knew the right words to cheer me up. And later that evening I would remember her words so clearly, because that Thursday would soon become the worst day of my ten years on Earth.

*

My life began to fall apart while I was sitting at the kitchen table, eating alphabet spaghetti and watching Countdown. I'm not very good at Countdown but I *do* like the clock music.

Then Mum came in. Black make-up tears ran down her face, so I knew something was up.

"Jeremy," she said, sniffling. "I need you to sit down for a minute."

"I am sitting down," I said.

She picked up the remote and turned off the TV, which was annoying because I'd just found a five-letter word — my best score ever. I didn't complain though because I could see Mum was upset. And what she said next made everything go swirly. I think I nearly fainted but I can't properly remember.

"Your dad and I are getting a divorce. He's moved out already and is buying a house on the other side of town. You'll still see him at weekends."

My throat felt sore and my lips started to quiver as I tried not to cry. It made no sense. Mum and Dad loved each other. They always had and they always would... until the end of time... that's what I'd thought anyway.

So, what had changed?

To stop myself from being sick, I focused on my watch. 16:13, said the screen. Thirteen minutes past four. I watched it, willing it to reverse so that Mum could take back those words and never repeat them. I picked at the strap, forcing back the tears. But the screen didn't change. 16:13. Thirteen minutes past four. And Mum didn't take back her words.

*

Later, upstairs, I found Dad's wardrobe empty.

It was true. He'd gone.

I couldn't stop the crying now. Tears drenched my face and snot dripped from my nose. I told Mum that I hated her. This was all her fault.

"Dad wouldn't leave unless you made him!" I screamed. I called her a cow and a pig and other animals too.

"You're just a... stupid otter!"

Not sure where that one came from.

I sobbed into my bed sheets for a long, long time.

Then I gazed out of the window for ages, just staring at trees and walls and fences. Wishing, hoping, praying that this was all a bad dream and I'd soon wake up.

I pinched myself. That's what people on the telly do to wake themselves up if they think they're in a dream.

I didn't wake up.

Staring at Mrs Patel's fence next door, I was reminded of Fanny's final flight, over the fence and into the toolbox. My poor little pet.

And then a thought hit me. An idea began bubbling in my mind. I thought about the way that things had altered over the past week or so. And then it became clear in my head, like a vision. I could see the problem solving itself in my mind. And half a smile turned up at the corner of my lips as I understood exactly how to get Dad back to our house... so that we could be a proper family again.

CHAPTER TWO:
YOU CAN'T MAKE AN OMELETTE WITHOUT BREAKING (CROCODILE) EGGS

A FAMILY ISN'T COMPLETE WITHOUT A PET!

The mystic tea towel was absolutely right. Like a great detective, I put the events of my family life in chronological order, which means in the order they happened. Miss Hope taught us that word. Chronological. It's one of my *Top Five Favourite Words*.

Once I'd created my mini timeline, the problem was crystal clear. I felt like a genius detective; smarter than Sherlock Holmes and Tintin and whatever the dog was called in *Scooby Doo*.

First, Mum and Dad are perfectly fine and happily married. Then, my pet goldfish throws herself out of a window and dies next to a B&Q screwdriver. After that, Dad moves out and everything starts falling to pieces. Coincidence? I think not!

What was it that Miss Hope said?

Looking after animals fills your heart with kindness and love.

Without a pet to care for, the love had emptied from my parents' hearts. Now I was facing life without a dad.

Unless.

Maybe — just maybe — if we had a new pet, perhaps Mum and Dad would rediscover their love for each other and everything would go back to normal.

*

The next evening, I asked Mum to buy me a new goldfish. I even told her that it would help; that it would stop her and Dad from falling out. But she said it was out of the question.

"We can't go buying new animals willy-nilly," she said as she got our dinner ready. For me, she'd cooked a chicken fillet with mashed potato and vegetables. I smiled at the broccoli on my plate. Broccoli was my favourite. My best friend Michael thinks it's evil.

For herself, Mum had a cracker covered in Philadelphia cheese.

"I'm not even sure we can still live here, Jeremy. There's so much to sort out with the divorce. So no, you're not having a new goldfish. I've got too much on my plate."

I looked down at her cracker and cheese.

"You've hardly got anything on your plate!" I said.

If only she could see that a new pet was the answer! Then she wouldn't need to go through with the stupid divorce. We could be happy again. A new pet would definitely save their marriage. Definitely. It was the best idea I'd ever had.

*

"That's the stupidest idea I've ever heard!"

My best friend Michael had never known his dad. His mum came to England from Ghana when he was just three months old. (And she didn't bring Michael's dad with her.) So Michael had never known what it was like to have two parents. It was obvious that he wouldn't understand my plan.

"Trust me," I said. "Pets bring families together. I know what I'm talking about. I saw it on a tea towel."

"A tea towel?"

I waved this away. "Forget it."

After school, Mum let me play on the park until half four. I had a digital Casio watch to keep track of the time. But today we weren't going to the park at all.

We crossed the market place in town, carefully avoiding the two homeless men arguing over a Greggs sausage roll. A big gang of pigeons were furiously pecking away at some chips on the floor near the telephone box.

After Mum had refused to buy me a goldfish, I'd come up with a new plan.

Opposite the market square, between ***Something's Not Right*** (a shop dedicated to left-handed equipment — golf clubs, scissors, pens) and ***Curl Up & Dye*** (a hairdressers for wrinkly old women) stood our town's only pet store. It was just two doors away ***The Pickled Liver*** pub.

Letchkov's Store: Pet Food, Pets and Non-Pets had quite a reputation. Apparently, you could buy all sorts in there.

Gorillas, guns, government-banned gadgets. If you needed it, Mr Letchkov could find it.

For this reason, Dad had never let me go in.

"Letchkov is a dirty foreigner," he said. "He's up to no good. They come over here from Transylvania, taking all our jobs. It's a disgrace!"

I hated it when Dad talked like that.

"I didn't know you wanted to work in a pet shop, Dad," I'd replied.

Dad tutted and told me I was too young to 'get it'. I told him that Mr Letchkov was actually from Bulgaria, not Transylvania (Letchkov's son was in my class at school — I really liked him).

Not that I cared where the man was from, or what he was 'up to'. As long as he could sell me a pet to save my parents' marriage, that was all I cared about.

*

"Right," I said to Michael as we stood outside the shop. "I've got the thirty pounds from my piggy bank. But I'm saving for a glow-in-the-dark Nerf gun, so I can only spend five pounds on a pet. Not a penny more."

Michael nodded.

A bell tinkled as we entered. I saw Mr Letchkov stubbing out a fag. The store reeked of cigarette smoke, hay and animal poo.

On the wall in front of us hung a selection of *'Non-Pets'*. Three samurai swords, a collection of harpoons and something called a *Dodgy Box 6000* ("See tomorrow's movies, before they're in the cinema!").

As we made our way around the dimly-lit store, it quickly became clear that this was no ordinary pet shop. There were no dogs, no hamsters, no cute little bunnies. The only cat in there had one ear, one eye and — judging by the desperate look of fear on his face — only one of his nine lives remaining.

I soon realised that five pounds wouldn't get me very far either. I couldn't afford any of the snakes or the giant turtles or the anteater. I couldn't afford a piranha or a mountain goat or a koala cub. I couldn't even afford the mangy old cat.

"You want to buy pet?" Mr Letchkov's voice made us both jump. He'd moved silently from behind his counter, bringing with him a whiff of stale cigarettes. He spoke with a strong

14

Bulgarian accent. "I do you good price on crocodile eggs. Very rare. Just ninety nine pounds."

"Sorry," I said. "I don't have *that* much money." Not that I thought a crocodile was the ideal pet to bring my parents back together.

"Okay. Here," said Mr Letchkov, shoving a massive egg into my hands. "Now you feel how special are these eggs. Very rare. Final offer. Seventy five pounds. Buy one, get one free."

"Sorry," I repeated, trying to give him back the egg. "I'm not sure that I want a –"

"Okay! You drive hard bargain. Fifty pounds. Buy one, get three free."

"Sorry. But I don't have much money. Let me show you."

Taking one hand away from the egg, I pulled out my wallet. As I did so, Mr Letchkov raised his hand. He nudged my elbow, causing me to lose grip of the crocodile egg, which soared to the ground. Before I could say 'sorry' one more time, the egg had smashed on the floor, leaving an explosion of shell and goo.

My stomach lurched. My heart was beating faster than a pneumatic drill.

I was a murderer! I'd killed a baby croc!

And Mr Letchkov looked like he was about to murder me!

"This very bad," he roared. "You pay for broken egg."

I held up my wallet. "I'm so sorry, Mr Letchkov. I only have thirty pounds and I'm saving for a glow-in-the-dark Nerf gun."

Letchkov grabbed the wallet and removed my money.

"This not enough. I ring police."

My heart skipped a beat. Getting arrested wasn't part of the plan.

Letchkov held up my three ten-pound notes.

"Okay. I let you off. Leave now. But if you ever come back, I want twenty more."

He held out my wallet for me to take. Without saying a word, I grabbed it and ran out of the shop with Michael.

*

We stood in an alley that stunk of wee. My eyes had filled with tears. Guilt churned in my gut. I'd murdered an unborn crocodile.

"It wasn't your fault," said Michael. "You know that, don't you?"

"What do you mean?" I said, sniffling.

"Letchkov nudged your arm. On purpose. I saw him. It wasn't your fault. And I don't think it was even a real crocodile egg. The floor was covered in yoke. Do crocodile eggs have yoke in them?"

"I have no idea."

I didn't. But Michael's words strengthened me. Thinking about it, I remembered that Letchkov *had* nudged me. Was this a scam to get money from innocent people?

A charge of anger ran through me. I felt more annoyed than when the school dinners ran out of turkey twizzlers last Tuesday.

I wanted to march back in there and demand my thirty pounds back — but Letchkov would never give it to me. Plus, I didn't have the guts to try. And anyway, as we made our way home for tea, Michael told me about a much more interesting — more dangerous — idea he'd had.

CHAPTER THREE: PRAT BURGLARS

I was more scared than a one-legged chicken in a cage full of lions. My knees had turned to jelly.

This was the naughtiest thing I'd done since the school Christmas party when Mrs Gillott, the portly Year Three teacher, said that we could only have one cup of Ribena, but I rejoined the queue twice more and ended up having three.

After tea, Michael and I were both allowed to play out until half six. We immediately returned to Pee-Stink alley and watched the pet shop. The two homeless men had gone from the market place but the pigeons were still pecking at chips and bits of newspaper. They'd completely destroyed the photo of the girl in a bikini from page three.

When Letchkov came out, my Casio said it was 17:13, which meant almost quarter past five. He locked the door, scratched his bum (very aggressively) and then left. This gave us just over an hour to get the job done.

Michael tried to reassure me that everything would be okay. He told me he did this sort of thing all the time.

"I nicked a motorbike two weeks ago," he claimed.

I'm pretty sure that this wasn't true. Michael had a terrible habit of making things up to make himself sound a lot tougher than he really was. He once told me that when he lived in Ghana, a hippo came into his house one day and he had to fight it off with a wooden spoon… he left Ghana when he was three months old, don't forget.

"Motorbikes are easy though," he added. "You just jump on and ride off."

I don't think this is true either. Still, his bullish confidence made me feel braver.

Down Pee-Stink alley, you could get to the rear end of the shops – the uglier side of the buildings that shoppers didn't usually see. Michael said it would be easier to do it on this side. No people, no cameras.

We climbed over a small wall into the backyard of Letchkov's store. My legs felt weak and my heart was hammering with fear.

"We shouldn't be doing this," I said.

Michael shook his head. "We *have* to do this. Letchkov thinks he can trick people. He thinks he can bully kids into giving him money. He thinks that nobody can touch him." Michael pointed at the shop as he spoke. "You said that you need a pet to save your parents' marriage. But Letchkov took your money. Every last penny you had. Are you just going to let him get away with it? Are you just going to let your parents get divorced?"

Michael had a good point. Still, I was unsure.

"No... but this isn't right."

Michael moved closer to me. His voice became a low hiss.

"When Hitler invaded Portugal, did the British people just lie down and surrender?"

I frowned with confusion. "You can't compare Mr Letchkov to Hitler," I said. "And I don't think Hitler actually invaded Por—"

"No!" Michael was on a roll now. "Britain stood up for what was right, what was fair. And that's what we need to do now. Stand up to Letchkov. Teach him a lesson."

Maybe Michael was right. Letchkov couldn't just go around taking money from innocent children. Someone had to stop him… even if it meant breaking the law.

I nodded at Michael and approached to the shop's back door. Nervousness twisted in my tummy as I tried the handle.

"It's locked," I stated.

"Of course it's locked, you dumbo," said Michael. "You need to go through there."

He pointed to a narrow window above the door and then pulled a wheelie bin over. Its wheels made a racket loud enough to wake up every animal inside the shop. I froze for a moment, expecting someone to come and investigate the noise. But nobody did.

Michael gave me a leg-up onto the bin and I stood up. My legs felt unsteady as the wheelie bin wobbled. This didn't feel like an operation by master criminals. We were more like prat burglars than cat burglars.

I tried to open the window. "It's locked."

"Of course it's locked," Michael repeated, whispering now. "That's why I brought this." He handed me a metal coat hanger.

I shook my head. "I'll keep my jacket on, thanks. It's dropped a bit cool."

Michael tutted. "No. You use it to jimmy the lock. That's how I got into Buckingham Palace."

"You broke into Buckingham Palace?"

"Yes. I went round the back, climbed on a wheelie bin and jimmied the lock with a coat hanger."

"You never told me this. What did you do inside?"

"I nicked one of the Queen's socks, but then I left it on the bus. Anyway, start jimmying the window before someone comes."

Now, before I go any further, let me please assure you that I only had good intentions here. Mr Letchkov had conned me out of thirty pounds (all the money I had in the world) and I couldn't let him get away with that. I didn't want to get the money back but I *did* want to get something else.

The mangy old cat with one eye and one ear had looked more suicidal than Fanny the fish, breathing in Mr Letchkov's cigarette smoke, surrounded by snakes and piranhas. And nobody was ever going to buy a nearly-dead cat from this store, especially at Letchkov's prices. So, I intended to save the half-blind cat, and — more importantly — save my parents' marriage.

Okay, so breaking into a shop and stealing a disabled cat may have been against the law, but I was *definitely* doing the right thing. Wasn't I?

There wasn't even the slightest gap in the window frame. I couldn't see anywhere that the coat hanger would go in. Maybe I didn't want to see a gap, not really. Maybe I wasn't looking properly. Maybe I just wanted to go home and forget about this whole situation, instead of breaking the law like a Class-A criminal. My nerves were frazzled with fear as I tried to steady my legs on the wobbly wheelie bin. I almost jumped out of my skin when a dog barked in the distance.

"How do you actually 'jimmy' a lock?" I asked Michael.

He looked up at me from the ground. "Well… you just jimmy a lock."

Helpful.

I tried again. "It's no good. I can't see a way in."

The next voice I heard was one that I recognised… but it wasn't Michael's.

I knew that it wasn't Michael's for three reasons.

1. It wasn't Michael's voice.
2. It was a woman.
3. It was my mum's friend, Jade.

She was a police officer.

"A way into where?" said the voice of my mum's friend, Jade the police officer.

My stomach flipped like it did when Dad drove over bridges too fast. Jade was wearing her uniform and everything. I felt sick and not just because the wheelie bin had rocked me around like a sailing boat in the middle of an ocean storm.

"We-we… We were just…"

"Seeing if the shop was open." Michael finished my bumbling sentence.

Jade, who had thick pouting lips, did not look impressed. She told me to get down from the bin and give her the coat hanger.

She marched us to her police car, where we were made to sit in the back seat like a pair of crooks.

I started to panic. Did we have criminal records now? What if Miss Hope walked past and saw us? She'd never let me near the snails again. What would Mum say? What would Dad say? I'd be grounded until I was thirteen at least... if I was out of prison by then!

Jade — or PC Jackson as she called herself on duty — gave us a long lecture. She told us how incredibly stupid we'd been and how much trouble we *should* have been in.

ATTEMPTED BURGLARY.
TRESPASSING.
CARRYING A DANGEROUS WEAPON.

Those were just three of the charges she could have arrested us for, though I didn't *really* see the coat hanger as a dangerous weapon. I wanted to tell Jade that Mr Letchkov had conned me and taken my Nerf Gun money. But she looked like she was in no mood for a debate so I kept quiet.

"I know you're both good kids," she said, looking deadly serious. "And I know that you both come from good families. If your parents heard about this, they'd be devastated." She paused for a moment, pouting her thick lips. They were covered with shiny lipstick.

"So," she said. "Seeing as you've never been in trouble before, on this one occasion I'm going to keep my mouth zipped. But if anything like this happens again, I'll have to take you down to the station."

At that moment, I felt so relieved. It was the kind of relief you get when you go for a wee after holding it in for a really long time. Still, my heart continued to pound as Jade drove us home. She dropped Michael off first – around the corner from his house so that his mum wouldn't see him getting out of a police car. I thought this was a nice thing to do.

After Michael had gone, Jade started talking again.

"Listen Jeremy. I know that you're upset about your mum and dad's divorce."

"I'm pretty sure that they'll get back together," I said.

"Hmmm…" Jade didn't sound convinced. "Well," she said. "Whatever happens, try not to blame your dad too much. Things have been… difficult… for him."

This took me by surprise. "Dad? No, I blame Mum. I know she's your friend and everything but it's all her fault. Dad would never move out and leave me unless she made him."

"Well…" Jade looked like she was about to say something but then didn't.

As I sat there, satisfied that I wasn't going to prison, I suddenly realised how good Jade smelled. I was almost certain that she wore the same perfume as Miss Hope, yet somehow it smelled even better on Jade. And I noticed for the first time that she was really attractive too. Not in a pretty pinky princess way, but her eyes sparkled, her lips shone and her nose was cute.

"Look Jeremy," she said eventually, as we pulled up around the corner from our house. "My parents broke up when I was around your age, so I know how tough it can be. Promise me that you'll stay out of trouble."

I promised that I would and climbed out of the car. Mr Clifford, one of our neighbours, was out in his garden. I was worried he'd see me with the police, but he was too busy organising his gnomes to notice.

Then, just as I was walking away, Jade opened her window.

"And remember," she said. "Don't be too hard on your dad."

Weird. I'd already told her it was Mum's fault. Why would I be hard on Dad? It didn't matter though. I knew that Mum and Dad would stay together, although I wasn't sure where I'd get a pet from now. I had no money and was banned from the only pet shop in town.

But a pet would bring them back together, I was certain. I sprinted quickly around the corner and over to our house. Mr Clifford never turned round to see me. Only his gnomes had their eyes on me. Luckily though, they usually kept quiet.

CHAPTER FOUR:
A FROG DRIVING
A SPORTS CAR

I'd wanted to see Dad over the weekend but Mum said he was too busy trying to buy this new house. I didn't see how hard it could be to buy a house. Just pick the one you like and pay for it. Simple. Mum said it was more complicated than that, so I didn't get to see him at all.

On Monday Miss Hope started teaching us about Henry the Eighth. Did you know that he had *six wives* in total? Sometimes he just got bored with them so he had their heads chopped off or he divorced them. Back then, divorce was illegal too. I wished it was illegal now. Henry the Eighth didn't care though. He just changed the laws to suit himself.

Everyone in class loved him because he was big and powerful and he just did whatever he wanted.

I didn't love him.

I thought he was a greedy, selfish pig. And he was clearly overweight.

"Do you think Miss Hope's getting fat?" whispered Michael as we sat in class, designing our own Tudor castle for Henry to live in.

"*Fat?*" I said, much too quickly. "No way!" Even though I *had* noticed she'd put on a bit of weight around her face and she *had* got a bit of a round pot-belly, I didn't like hearing anyone call her fat. Henry the Eighth was fat, not Miss Hope.

"Well I think she is," said Michael. "And she's stopped drinking coffee too. Have you noticed that?"

I hadn't. But when I looked over, sure enough, Miss Hope *was* holding her belly, sipping a bottle of mineral water. Maybe she was on a new diet that didn't involve drinking coffee. Maybe she'd started going to Weight Wobblers like Mum (Mum only started because Dad made her).

"Anyway," said Michael — after we'd decided where in our Tudor castle to put the blacksmith. "I went on Facebook last night. There's a page on there called ***Local Pets For Sale***."

"Yeah, well, perhaps you forgot, I don't have any money to buy a pet. Mr Letchkov took my last penny."

Michael waved this away. "There's a guy on there. Victor Singh. He's giving pets away for free."

I arched an eyebrow. "Free? What's the catch?"

"There's no catch. You just have to take a selfie with one of the animals and post it on Instagram."

I wasn't allowed to have Facebook or Instagram. I wasn't even allowed a phone. Dad said it wasn't safe because there could be predators out there. I couldn't understand why lions or great white sharks would be interested in an iphone. Anyway, Michael had the lot; Tweetspace, Instaface, Snapsapp.

"Is it safe?" I said. "To visit this Mr Singh?"

Michael shrugged. "Probably. He says the first five people to post selfies get a free pet. It's to help promote his taxidermy."

"What's taxidermy?" I asked.

"I guess he helps people with their taxes. My mum is always complaining that she doesn't understand how taxes work."

That made perfect sense to me.

So, after school, we found the address for ***Singh's Taxidermy*** and set off on our bikes.

*

As soon as Victor Singh answered the door, we realised that he wasn't exactly… normal.

Mr Singh ran his taxidermy business from his home, a cosy-looking bungalow just three streets away from my house. We set our bikes down, knocked on the door and waited. I wondered what sort of pet I could take home. Something fluffy would save my parents' marriage for certain. Maybe a cute bunny or a tiny kitten.

After a few moments, we heard a man approaching on the other side of the door. He was whistling merrily. What we saw when he opened the door was something of a surprise.

Mr Singh was an oldish Asian man, roughly seventy years old. He had a bushy, white beard invading his entire face — but he was completely bald, as if he'd put his head on upside-down. He wore a yellow Hawaiian shirt, covered with parrots and palm trees. Not quite the tax expert we'd expected.

"Hello," I said. "Are you Victor Singh?"

A mischievous grin stretched across his face. "That'll be my name until the fat lady… Singhs! Geddit?" He then burst into fits of giggles. Michael and I just looked at each other.

"We've come about your advert," I said. "Something about a free pet?"

"Oh yes!" Mr Singh chuckled again. "Come in, come in. Welcome to Barkingham Palace. Geddit? Bark-ingham Palace." He then gave out a great belly-laugh.

We stepped into the house. Other than Mr Singh's laughing and the sound of a ticking clock, the house was quiet. He'd called it Barkingham Palace but I couldn't hear any barking… or meowing… or whatever sound it was that rabbits made. I couldn't help but wonder what sorts of pets he was giving away.

Mr Singh showed us into his old-fashioned living room, where we sat on the sofa. The house smelled like an old museum, fusty and dusty.

"Now, did you bring a camera?" Mr Singh asked, looking serious for the first time. "Because I need you to take a photo with one of the animals first. It's to help promote my taxidermy business."

Michael held up his phone. "Yes. Got it here."

"Fantastic!" The big grin returned to Mr Singh's face. "I'll go and get the animals for a photo." His bright Hawaiian shirt then disappeared out of the room.

Michael turned to look at me. "He's bonkers," he whispered.

I nodded. "Let's just take the photo, get the free pet and get out of here."

Moments later, Mr Singh came back in the room, carrying a gigantic trunk. It looked like a pirate's treasure chest. He placed it on the floor next to the coffee table in the middle of the room. The lid opened towards us, so we couldn't see what creatures were inside. The anticipation was killing me.

"Okay," said Mr Singh excitedly. "I'll put them on the table and you can choose your animal for the selfie. And don't forget, you need to put hash-brown *Singh's Taxidermy*."

"Do you mean *hash-tag*?" asked Michael.

"That's the one," said Mr Singh, giggling wildly. "Okay. Here's my favourite." He reached into the treasure chest and then placed the most bizarre thing on the table that I'd ever seen.

Have you ever seen a frog driving a sports car?

No?

Well, I hadn't either until I visited ***Singh's Taxidermy.***

Okay, so the car wasn't a real car. It was some sort of model Porsche, a soft-top about the size of a small toaster. But the frog was definitely real. It wasn't a toy. It wasn't a robot. It was a REAL frog.

Yes, it was dead — definitely dead — so I'm guessing it had been stuffed.

"What happens when the car breaks down?" said Mr Singh, biting his lip, barely able to contain his laughter. "He gets TOAD away! Geddit? He's a toad!"

Michael and I nodded, unsure what to make of the situation.

Mr Singh dived into his box and pulled out a second monstrosity. This animal was much bigger and took up a lot more space on the coffee table. It was a stuffed sheep, standing on its hind legs, dressed in a karate outfit (black belt). The sheep's eyes had a look of anger in them, as if it had died in the middle of a fight. I was starting to get a bit scared.

"Guess what his special move is," said Mr Singh, who was was clearly more bonkers than I'd first thought. "Lamb chop! Geddit? Because it's a lamb doing karate."

I nodded again. "Yep. I get it."

The third animal from the treasure chest was a stuffed dog, a Dalmatian. It wasn't doing anything crazy, like flying a plane or fixing a radiator. It was just a normal Dalmatian (if you could called a stuffed dog 'normal'), mostly white and covered in black spots.

"Why can't this dog play hide and seek?" Mr Singh asked.

Michael and I shrugged, wondering when this was ever going to end.

"Because she's always spotted! Geddit?" Mr Singh roared with laughter.

We didn't.

This went on for a while. Loads of weird stuffed animals: a fox wearing boxing gloves, a mole drinking a can of beer and so on. They would always be followed by a terrible joke from Mr Singh.

Once they were all on display, we were asked which one we'd like to have our photo with.

"It's to help promote my taxidermy business," said Mr Singh once more.

"Okay," I said, finally getting up from the sofa. "But what do dead animals have to do with taxes?"

Mr Singh stared at me for a long moment as if I was talking an alien language. And then he suddenly burst into a gigantic scream of laughter.

"HA HA HA! That's brilliant! I'll have to remember that one! Taxes!"

What was he laughing at? Why didn't he answer my question? This time, I *didn't* 'get it' at all. I looked at Michael. Judging by the confused look on his face, neither did he.

We quickly decided on a stuffed animal for a selfie. We picked a badger reading a book — *Fantastic Mr Fox* by Roald Dahl. Singh made sure that Michael then uploaded the photo to Instagram.

#SinghsTaxidermy

"Brilliant," said Mr Singh. "I'll go and fetch a pet for you to choose."

Just when I thought things couldn't get any weirder, they did.

The five pets that Mr Singh was willing to give away were not quite what I'd been expecting… and they certainly weren't going to help bring my parents back together.

A rat wearing an Arsenal kit.

A mouse playing a ukulele.

A gerbil using a typewriter.

A shrew mending a shoe.

A vole playing golf.

All dead.

All stuffed.

"So all of the animals here are dead?" I asked.

"Of course," said Mr Singh. "Stuffed animals are so much easier to take care of. They don't leave dirty mess on your carpet. They don't wake you up in the middle of the night for a wee. They don't squawk or scream or squeal." Mr Singh giggled. "Now, let me give you a few minutes to decide which pet you want while I go to the kitchen and fetch you a special treat."

A flash of beard and bright shirt then zoomed out of the room. Michael grabbed my arm.

"We need to get out of here," he said. "This geezer is sooooo weird!"

I had to agree.

Dead animals?

What the heck?

But I didn't just want to leave without saying goodbye, that would be rude.

Michael moved for the door. "Didn't you hear what he said? He prefers thing to be dead. He means us! His 'special treat' is probably a poisonous drink or… or… a machine gun!"

The hairs on my neck suddenly stood up. I felt my stomach twist. Michael was probably right. We had to leave.

We bolted from the room and out of the house. We grabbed our bikes and peddled like mad, away from Mr Singh's bungalow.

As we turned the corner, I spotted Mr Singh standing at his front door. I heard his voice. It sounded small and confused.

"Where are you going? You forgot to take a pet. I've got some Hobnob biscuits for you."

When I got home, I searched the internet.

Taxidermy — it turns out — has nothing to do with taxes. It is the art of *'stuffing animals for lifelike effect'*.

CHAPTER FIVE:
EATING FOR TWO

Giant African Land Snails are hermaphrodites.

I love that word. Hermaphrodite. Along with 'chronological', it's definitely in my list of *Top Five Favourite Words.*

A hermaphrodite is a person (or animal, in this case) who is both male and female at the same time.

My Uncle Tony says that he's a woman trapped in a man's body, but I think that's different. Dad won't let me see Uncle Tony any more, says he a freak, which is a shame because I really love Uncle Tony.

Anyway, I know loads of other facts about Giant African Land Snails. They can grow up to twenty centimetres long, which is pretty massive for a snail (two-thirds of a ruler!).

The foods they like best are cucumbers and lettuce. Sometimes if there's salad for school dinner, I save some lettuce for Pea and Pod.

You can also feed them bananas but you have to take the banana out before it turns brown because brown bananas give them diarrhoea.

On Tuesday I'd taken a packed lunch to school for a change. Miss Hope asked me to feed the snails with her at dinner time. She said I could eat my sandwiches with her in class. Some people might think this was a date, but we're just good friends.

Miss Hope drank only water (no coffee) and ate *loads* for lunch. She said she was 'eating for two', which I didn't understand because I ate all of my food myself (corned beef butties and a packet of Quavers — if you're interested).

"I heard about your mum and dad's separation," she said, picking out a slice of cucumber from her sandwich.

I said that they probably weren't going to get divorced and then told her my plan to get a pet. "Remember," I said, "you told me that looking after animals fills your heart with kindness and love. We just need a new pet and they'll get back together. Definitely."

Miss Hope frowned. "Jeremy, I didn't mean that a pet would save your parents' marriage. I know that it's difficult to hear but your plan might not work. If your parents want a divorce, then

I'm sorry to say that it's likely to happen." She sighed and then dropped the slice of cucumber into the tank for the snails. "What sort of pet are you thinking of getting?"

I was unsure what to tell her. I didn't want to include any details about my new criminal lifestyle.

"Well... I wanted something fluffy, but I, erm... *lost*... all my money. So now I'm not sure. It needs to be an animal that's alive, that's for certain."

Miss Hope arched an eyebrow. "I don't think you can get dead pets, Jeremy."

"You'd be surprised," I said. "Anyway, Michael reckons we could try and catch a wild animal and tame it. Says he tamed a tiger when he lived in Ghana."

Miss Hope squinted. "I don't think that's true."

"It's not," I said. "Tigers don't even live in Ghana. I looked it up on Wikipedia. Plus, he was only three months old when he lived there."

"So, what sort of animal were you thinking of catching?" she asked, biting on her sandwich.

"A swan," I said.

Miss Hope nearly choked on her lunch. Her voice became a screech. "A *swan?*"

I nodded. "Gary the deaf swan has some cygnets nesting near Foster Pond. Michael says we could take one. He reckons he shot a swan once."

Miss Hope looked confused. "Gary the deaf swan?"

"Yeah. It's this swan that's really aggressive and really loud. Everyone reckons he's deaf. That's why he's so loud. So they called him Gary the deaf swan. Then he laid some eggs and they realised that Gary was a girl."

Miss Hope shook her head. "Jeremy, I think that taking a baby swan away from its mother is a really bad idea. It's dangerous and I'm pretty sure it's illegal."

"Yeah, that's what I said. Michael reckons that swans can break your arm. There's no way that I'm messing with a giant Kung-Fu duck."

I reached into the snails' tank and lifted Pod out of the soil. I knew it was Pod because his shell was lighter than Pea's. I gave the shell a stroke. I'm not sure if he could feel it, but it made *me* feel better.

"I thought I could perhaps catch a hedgehog. That would make a good pet. But they don't come on our garden, we've got crazy paving. And I'm not allowed out after dark. Hedgehogs are nocturnal, aren't they?"

Miss Hope nodded. Pod slimed across my hand. She had a worried look on her face – Miss Hope, not Pod. I wasn't sure if it was because she was worried that I'd do something silly with a wild animal… or because she was about to tell me yet another piece of terrible news.

I placed Pod back in the tank, right next to the sliced cucumber. Miss Hope and I washed our hands at the sink and then dried them with paper towels.

"Will you look after the snails while I'm away?" said Miss Hope.

This took me by surprise.

"Away? What do you mean?"

"Haven't you noticed?" Miss Hope patted her round belly. "I'm pregnant. I'll be off school for a while."

My jaw practically fell to the floor. I couldn't believe it. First Fanny had gone from my life, then Dad, now Miss Hope. My whole world was crumbling around me.

"Pregnant?" I said. "I didn't even know you were married!"

Miss Hope laughed. "People don't have to married to have children. But, as a matter of fact, I *am* getting married this weekend. By Saturday night, I'll have changed from Miss Hope to Mrs Bunyan."

"Mrs Bunyan?!" Now *my* voice was a screech. "That's a stupid name!"

I didn't care if I'd offended her. This wasn't fair! How could she just leave me?

"How long will you be off for?" I asked.

"I'm allowed thirty nine weeks off, but I think I'm going to take a full year off. Start school afresh next September."

"*Next* September?!" My voice had become really high-pitched. "But… but… I'll have gone to secondary school by then!"

"I'll come back and visit before you leave."

"So when are you leaving to have this baby?" I asked.

Miss Hope gave me a sad smile. "This Friday."

"What?!" I felt a lump in my throat. Tears were forming at the corners of my eyes. The end of my world was approaching fast. Miss Hope would soon be no more. And I felt all hope in my life slipping away.

CHAPTER SIX:
FLOYD

Miss Hope — soon to be Mrs Bunyan (yuck!) — was always out of class on Thursday afternoons. It was her time to do marking and stuff. I don't know why she couldn't just do it all at home after school. It wasn't like teachers had a life.

Mrs Kapoor, a teaching assistant, usually taught us art and then RE, which stands for Religious Education — but Michael and I called it Rubbish Explanations. Today though, we were making 'Good Luck' cards for Miss Hope. People were drawing babies and flowers on their cards but I couldn't be bothered.

On my first go, I just wrote:

To Miss Hope, I hate you. Jeremy Green.

But I threw it in the bin before Mrs Kapoor told me off.

"What do you think our new teacher will be like?" asked Michael, who'd drawn a picture of a pregnant Miss Hope on his card. It looked more like a whale with legs.

I shrugged. "Dunno. I bet she'll be nicer than Miss Hope."

Michael stopped drawing and looked at me. "I thought you loved Miss Hope?"

I shook my head. "Nah. Did you know that she's going to be called Mrs Bunyan?"

"Ha!" said Michael. "Onion." He carried on with his drawing, colouring the sky blue. "What if we get a man teacher? That would be so cool! We could just play football and cricket all day."

"I don't think that's how it works," I said.

*

After school, I was annoyed to see that Auntie Carol's BMW was parked outside our house. Not that I disliked Auntie Carol. Her son was the problem. My chubby cousin, Floyd, was more irritating than a Saturday-night TV talent shows.

Floyd was a year below me at school but he was about a foot taller and weighed twice as much. Mum said he was overweight because Auntie Carol couldn't cook properly. I said to Mum that he should go to *Weight Wobblers* with her. That was the last time I remember Mum laughing.

After we ate tea — and I watched Floyd greedily eat a second dessert — I wanted to meet up with Michael.

"You'll have to take Floyd with you then," said Auntie Carol. "I need to have a serious talk with your Mum." This meant they were going to sit around, saying horrible things about Dad.

"I want to play Playstation," said Floyd in a whiny voice.

"Tough," said Auntie Carol. "Out you go."

Floyd followed me outside, dragging his feet. We met Michael on the street corner. I told him that I was in a bad mood and felt like smashing something up. He said we could throw stones at the windows of Harkington Mill. It was in the middle of nowhere, so nobody would see us.

"That sounds naughty," said Floyd, the skin around his mouth covered in chocolate from his double helping of cake. "Are you going to get me into trouble?"

"No," I said, setting off in the direction of Harkington Mill.

"Do we have to walk there?" said Floyd, his voice whinier than ever.

"Well, seeing as I don't have a car, then yes."

Harkington Mill was an abandoned cotton mill on the edge of town. Last year in Miss Munroe's class, we learned about the local area. Apparently, the mill was built more than two hundred years ago and was once a busy, booming factory. Now it just stood there, looking old and ugly — like Miss Hope.

Floyd dragged himself slowly behind us like a disabled seal. The sky was already darkening by the time we arrived. Floyd was still way behind us.

"So," said Michael, looking for a decent rock to throw, "what are you going to do about this pet thing? I reckon we could easily catch a pigeon. I've done it before. Pigeons are idiots."

"Nah," I said, throwing a stone at the building and watching it miss all of the windows, bouncing back off the wall. "I think I've given up on pets. Too much trouble. I'm going to see my dad at the weekend. I'll just try and persuade him to do something. He can't just let Mum kick him out like that."

Floyd finally joined us, a good seven minutes after we'd arrived. He was panting and wheezing like an asthmatic donkey.

"My mum says that your dad is a rat," said Floyd, his breath rasping in his throat.

"Well, I don't care what you or your mum say," I told him.

Floyd giggled. He had a humorously high-pitched giggle for such a large kid.

"I was going to say," he laughed, "that your dad must love cheese!" His laugh then turned into a massive duck-like quack and I remembered how immature he was.

I sighed. His joke was stupid.

"Everyone loves cheese," I said. "That's just a well-known fact."

My next stone smashed straight through a window, causing an almighty crash to echo for miles. The sound of breaking glass hung in the air for a moment before it was slowly replaced by a second sound, the sound of an engine. Was it coming from inside the factory? Impossible. The place had been abandoned for more than a hundred years. Then the sound became louder and clearer, as if it was getting closer. I could also hear the sound of rolling tyres. It was coming from behind.

I was just about to turn my head when I heard Michael yell.

"L.A.P.D.!"

Approaching the mill was a police car. In the driver's seat, PC Jade Jackson. My heart skipped. I instinctively ran in the opposite direction.

"Come on, Floyd!" I yelled. *"Run!"*

Like a rhino on the charge, Floyd's tree-trunk legs suddenly kicked into gear. Glancing back, I saw every part of Floyd's flabby skin wobbling like the ripples of an ocean.

The police car still hadn't pulled up. They were way behind us, even with Floyd slowing us down. But we had to get out of there. I'd smashed a window. This would be my second offence. There was no way that Jade would let me off twice. I just hoped she hadn't seen our faces.

We darted past the factory building and paused on the other side for Floyd to catch up. When he joined us, he was gasping for air.

"Let's... hide... in the... building," he said.

"No way!" said Michael. "That place is haunted. I got chased in there once by a ghost that was carrying its own head."

At the rear of the factory, there was a crowd of trees and plants. Through them we could get to Foster Pond, which was right near the woods — a great place to escape. We darted through the tangled bushes — well, Floyd bulldozed through — before sprinting up a steep hill towards Foster Pond. We'd need to go around the pond to get into the woods.

I made it up the hill first and waited for the others. But that was when I realised I'd made a massive mistake.

Behind me, I heard the sound of hissing. Not any old hissing. This was angry, nasty hissing like a heavyweight snake in a championship wrestling match.

Only it wasn't a snake.

I turned around to see the biggest swan I'd ever seen in my life, hissing and spitting and ready to kill me.

"Gary the deaf swan!" yelled Michael as he soared past.

Like a giant Kung-Fu bird, the swan spread its huge wings to make itself look even bigger than ever. I stepped back and heard twigs snap beneath me. And that's when I realised why this massive bird was ready to fight.

I'd stepped on her nest.

Next to my feet were six grey cygnets. They looked just like ducklings, and — for a split second — I thought they'd be a brilliant pet to save my parents' marriage.

But then Gary charged. I dodged away, moving clear of the swan, before running towards the woods. Michael was ahead of me, Floyd almost caught up.

I thought I was in the clear when I suddenly felt the ground give way beneath me. I'd stepped on a loose rock. My left foot slipped. I fell, pressing all of my weight onto my ankle. A sharp charge of pain ran up my left leg.

I lay on the floor in agony as Floyd waddled past, his bum cheeks wriggling like a sack of ferrets.

"Floyd! Help me!"

Floyd ignored me, shuffling into the woods.

The pain in my left ankle killed. But I didn't have much time to think about it. Gary was still upset with me for stepping on her nest.

Pushing myself up, I managed to stand on my right leg. Gary made another fierce charge. Without a second's hesitation, I dodged out the swan's way. I turned, limped into the woods as fast as could and headed home.

For the first time in his life, Floyd was faster than me.

*

Floyd made it home much sooner than I did. He must have been a sweaty, blubbering mess when he got there. Exercise and getting in trouble were two of Floyd's least favourite things.

He told Mum everything.

Mum got very angry and grounded me for a week. Still, she noticed my leg and wanted to take me to hospital. I told her it was fine (even though it was killing like mad) but I couldn't go to the hospital.

Firstly, I knew that the police always hung around hospitals after major crimes like this. Was throwing stones at an old building a major crime? Probably. If they'd seen me fall on that loose rock, the hospital would be the first place they'd look.

Secondly, tomorrow was Miss Hope's last day. If I went to hospital, they might keep me in overnight. Normally, I would have loved a day off school, but not tomorrow. Even though

Miss Hope was ugly and I hated her, I wouldn't have missed her last day as my teacher for the world.

CHAPTER SEVEN: MRS SKARRATT

Thanks to my new limp, I got plenty of attention the next day. Lots of the girls were concerned, which felt pretty good, and Michael was on fine form.

"We were being chased by these older kids," he said, being careful not to mention the police. "Big, ugly teenagers they were. Then Jeremy was attacked by these massive swans! Three of them!"

Even Miss Hope acted like she cared, despite not caring enough to teach us for the rest of the year.

Her final morning as my teacher felt like any normal Friday, although lots of parents and staff brought her cards and presents. We did Maths and Literacy, and Miss Hope kept a smile on her face throughout.

It wasn't until the afternoon that things changed... things *really* changed.

"Right then children," said Miss Hope, once we'd all come in after lunch, "as you all know, today is my final day. So, for the rest of the year, you will have a new teacher."

Michael had his eyes closed and his fingers crossed. He was whispering.

"Please be a man! Please be a man!"

"Boys and girls," Miss Hope went on. "I'd like you all to meet your new teacher."

Thirty pairs of eyes watched with looks of panic, disgust and fear as our new teacher entered the class. In front of us stood a skinny old witch with a big hairy mole on the side of her nose. She looked back at us with small, suspicious eyes and a mouth as sour as a grapefruit. Hairs sprouted from her chin like a goatee beard.

Michael whispered to me. "Is that a man or not?"

"This is Mrs Skarratt," said Miss Hope.

"Ha!" Michael whispered. "Carrot."

This couldn't be right. The old woman looked like she knew more about casting spells and black cats than she did about teaching school children. I wouldn't have been surprised if she'd come to school on a broomstick.

"Right," said Miss Hope. "I'm going to leave you for half an hour to get to know each other." She gave the class a final smile before leaving us alone with scowling Mrs Skarratt.

As soon as Miss Hope left the room, a blonde girl named Amelia Stone put up her hand.

"Mrs Skarratt, can we make our Easter cards this afternoon?"

The new teacher, whose hair looked greasy and unwashed, glared at Amelia for a moment before speaking. Her voice was as bitter as an onion.

"Of course not, you little maggot," she hissed. "I HATE Easter… and Christmas and Halloween and Valentine's Day… and Monday and Tuesday and Wednesday and Thursday and Friday."

She paused for a moment to itch the hairy mole on her nose.

"I don't know what nonsense they've been teaching in this sad excuse for a school, but things are about to change. You!" She pointed a bony finger at Alfie Brown. "Stop slouching and sit up straight!" Alfie immediately did as the old crow told him. "Usually, schools aren't bad places," she said. "But there's always one thing that spoils 'em. Do any of you brats know what that thing is?"

Everyone stayed silent, sitting perfectly still (and now perfectly straight) in our chairs. Then Herbert Humphreys, the cleverest lad in our class, put up his hand. Mrs Skarratt let him give his answer.

"Is it an ever-increasing squeeze on funds by a government filled with politicians who are more interested in lining their own pockets than helping the less privileged?"

Herbert always talked about stupid stuff like that.

"No!" barked Mrs Skarratt. "The only problem with schools are the dirty, snifflin' germ-ridden kids!"

Everyone in class remained silent... until Michael whispered into my ear.

"The only thing germ-ridden is her!"

I couldn't help but chuckle. It was a mistake.

"You two!" Mrs Skarratt was now pointing in our direction. "What are you two gremlins laughing at?"

I didn't dare to speak. My tummy started doing nervous flips.

Michael was less scared. "I just wondered why you would have a school without kids?"

Mrs Skarratt stared at him with cold, fierce eyes as if she was trying to turn him to stone. "Cheeky little creature, aren't you?

You know what they do to cheeky children in some countries?" Her voice then became a dangerous whisper. "They would cut out their tongues so the little gits couldn't talk any more. And then they would eat their tongues with salt and vinegar for tea!"

Everyone in class looked terrified. Someone sounded like they were going to be sick. A couple of the girls made a whimpering sound.

"Unfortunately," Mrs Skarratt hissed, "they won't let me do that here. So you can have a lunchtime detention on Monday."

She pointed a skeletal finger at Michael. "And during that detention, you can clean my shoes."

At that moment, all thirty pairs of eyes looked down at Mrs Skarratt's feet. Her old boots were covered in mud. It looked like she'd walked through a cow field to get here. A faint whiff of manure drifted from their direction.

"And you!" The bony finger now pointed at me. "Laughing boy. You can join him. Monday lunchtime. One shoe each."

The thought of touching those old boots made me feel ill. But on the plus side, at least I'd be able to feed Pea and Pod while I was in here at lunch. Well, that's what I thought anyway. As it turned out, Mrs Skarratt had very different plans for the two snails.

At the end of the day, I left a card on Miss Hope's desk. I'd made it at home, after Mum sent me to my room for (nearly) getting Floyd arrested. On the front, I'd drawn a picture of me and Miss Hope holding hands, each walking a massive snail on a lead. I thought it looked really cool.

Inside I wrote:

To Miss Hope,

I am going to miss you so much. You are the best teacher I've ever had and I wish you could be my teacher forever. I promise to look after Pea and Pod while you are away.

Loads of love from

Jeremy Green

P.S. Please don't change your name to Mrs Bunyan. It's a stupid name.

P.P.S. Sorry that I called your new name stupid.

I left it on her desk and then left without saying goodbye. I couldn't say goodbye. It would've made me too upset. And I had a whole week of being upset still to come.

CHAPTER EIGHT: CHEAP AFTERSHAVE AND SWEAT

I couldn't wait to see Dad on Saturday. I'd missed him loads since he moved out. Plus, it would give me chance to persuade him to move back in and patch things up with Mum.

My ankle was still killing when I woke up on Saturday morning so Mum rang Dad and asked him to pick me up. Dad said that I was just being lazy, and Mum was already late for work, so I ended up limping across town on my own.

For the past week or so, Dad had been staying at his friend's Bed & Breakfast, *The Ponderosa*. It stood on the main road out of town and would normally have taken me about fifteen minutes to get there. Today though — hobbling like an old war veteran — the epic journey lasted almost half an hour.

As I eventually approached the place, my ankle hurting more than ever, I noticed something worrying. A police car was parked up outside. I immediately thought back to the other night, throwing stones at the windows of Harkington Mill.

I decided to wait a moment before going any further. I hid behind a red Vauxhall Corsa on the opposite side of the road, poking my head above the bonnet. I felt like a sniper or a detective, secretly staking out my target — the difference being, I was actually the one in hiding.

I stayed there for a few minutes and was about to make my move in to see Dad (mainly because I was bored) when something even worse happened.

PC Jade Jackson.

Coming out of the B&B where Dad was staying. A big dose of dread ran through my guts. If she'd been to see Dad, that could only mean one thing. She'd seen me throwing stones at Harkington Mill and had gone to tell Dad everything, about the mill *and* the pet store.

Mum had already grounded me for a month after Floyd had snitched on me. Dad was a trillion times worse when he was angry.

There was just one thought nagging at me.

Why had Jade gone to see Dad, not Mum?

I watched her get into her police car alone and drive off. I ducked behind the red Corsa as she drove past.

Then I looked at the B&B, took a deep breath and started to walk over. I tried to think of an excuse, a reason why I'd suddenly started behaving badly. I didn't want to blame Michael. That was a coward's way out. Plus, Dad already disliked my best friend for some unknown reason.

Then it hit me. I'd just tell the truth. I'd been upset about Mum and Dad splitting up. It would be the perfect way to start persuading Dad to move back home.

*

As I opened the front door, a bell tinkled above my head. *The Ponderosa* was just like someone's house, only it smelled of fried breakfast and strong coffee, and the carpet looked like it hadn't been hoovered in a year.

In front of me, a staircase led up to a higher floor, and on either side of me were doors. From somewhere in the back, a noisy radio blared; two men were discussing the big game between Chelsea and Spurs later that day.

At the sound of the bell, Dad's friend Paul appeared from the back. He asked me how I was 'keeping up' and tried to sound cheery, but I could tell from his eyes that he felt sorry for me. Maybe he'd even heard about my crimes from PC Jackson. After a bit of pointless small-talk, he told me that Dad was in room four, second on the right.

I made my way upstairs and then nervously knocked on the door.

Dad opened it wearing an old t-shirt with the name of his favourite band on the front, *Colin Wrist and the Baffled Wasps*. His face was unshaven with a silly grin plastered across it.

"Hey, I think you forgot your —" He stopped when he saw me. "Oh. Jeremy. I thought you were… Never mind. Come in." He pulled me in and gave me a massive hug. His room smelled like a mixture of cheap aftershave and sweat. "How have you been, little man?"

Although I didn't really like it when he called me 'little man' (I was third tallest in my class), I was pretty relieved. He didn't seem cross at all. In fact, he looked incredibly cheery to say that he was going through a divorce and he'd just found out that his son was now living a gangster lifestyle.

"What did the police want?" I blurted out, eager to know what had been said.

"The police?" said Dad, frowning.

The nervous bubble inside my guts eased a little. Maybe Jade hadn't been to see Dad after all. There were a million reasons why a police officer might need to visit *The Ponderosa,* Paul's pirate DVD collection being just one of them.

"Oh," I said. "I saw Mum's friend, Jade, the police woman. Just thought she might have been to see you."

Dad's eyes widened. "Erm," he hesitated for a moment. "Well... Yeah. She came to ask about your Mum."

I could tell that Dad was lying. But I didn't know why. Surely Jade would've gone to see Mum to ask her if she was okay. But, on the other hand, if she'd been here to tell Dad what I'd been up to, why wasn't he going mad?

Something smelled fishy, and it wasn't just Dad's dirty socks on the floor. We walked over to his unmade bed and sat down. The sheets stunk. I doubted they'd been changed since he'd been staying there. All sorts of things were scattered across the carpet; towels, t-shirts, empty packets of *Pickled Onion Monster Munch*. The dull room was depressing. I couldn't believe that Mum was forcing Dad to live here.

"So, what did you tell her?" I asked.

"Sorry?" Dad seemed surprised by my question.

"Mum," I said. "What did you tell Jade about Mum?"

Dad shrugged. "Oh, you know, the usual. Anyway, what about you, little man? Have you been okay?" He seemed keen to get away from the subject.

"Well, not bad," I said. "Our teacher left yesterday though, to have a baby."

"That's women for you," he said. "Unreliable. Which teacher? Mrs Gillott?"

I frowned. "I haven't had Mrs Gillott for two years. Anyway, we have this new teacher now, Mrs Skarratt. She's horrible. She gave me and Michael detention for laughing."

Dad nodded. "That's good. You shouldn't have been laughing at school. This Mrs Cabbage sounds like the kind of teacher you need. There's not enough discipline in schools these days."

Dad stood up from the bed, scratched his bum and then wandered over to a little table. He picked up a battered old kettle — that looked about as electrically safe as sticking wet fingers into a socket — and filled it with water at the bathroom sink.

"Want a cuppa?" he asked.

There were two mugs on the table, both stained brown inside. There were also two wine glasses, one had a lipstick mark on it. I guessed that Jade had drank water from it. She wouldn't have been drinking wine at this time in the morning.

"I'm okay thanks," I said, not fancying the dirty cups. "I'll just have a cold drink."

He clicked on the kettle and fetched me a glass of water.

"I can't believe you're still hanging around with that Michael kid," said Dad. "And now he's getting you in trouble at school."

"Michael's my best friend," I said.

"He's a waster," said Dad. "Where's he from again? Jamaica?"

"His Mum's from Ghana but she moved here when Michael was just a baby."

Dad tutted. I'm not sure why. He put a teabag and two spoonfuls of sugar in one of the dirty mugs. Clouds of steam started to rise from the rickety old kettle.

"Want to go and play football?" said Dad.

"If you like," I said, but immediately regretted it. There were a thousand other things I'd rather do than play football, especially with my injured ankle. Don't get me wrong, I do love football… but only watching. I'm rubbish at playing.

Dad signed me up for a team once, *Meadowbank Wolves* (only I played more like a chihuahua). My first game – and last game, as it turned out – didn't go well. The first time someone passed to me, I panicked and picked the ball up – and I wasn't playing in goal either. Handball. Penalty to the other team. I could tell that my teammates were annoyed.

In the second half, things got worse. I didn't realise that you changed ends at half time. So, I ran with the ball – I thought I was doing so well – and then smashed it into the goal. Then I realised that I'd scored past *our* goalkeeper. I'd been running the wrong way. Own goal.

This time, my teammates shouted at me. The manager subbed me off. Dad said he was embarrassed. I never played for *Meadowbank Wolves* again.

*

After getting dressed, Dad took me to the shop to buy a new football (top of the range — not that I cared). Then we went to the park for a knockabout. It had turned into a nice April day with plenty of sunshine.

Even though my ankle was killing and I kept slicing the ball all over the place, Dad seemed happy enough to be playing with me. So I felt that this was the right time to talk about Mum.

"I think Mum misses you," I said, after Dad had easily saved one of my shots.

He didn't answer. Just made a half-grunt/half-laugh sound.

"Why don't you move back home," I suggested. "It's nicer than the *Ponderosa*. Plus, Mum does your washing and ironing, and we could play football every day."

I didn't really want to play football every day, but I'd do it to save my parents' marriage.

Dad smiled with his mouth, but not with his eyes. His eyes held a deep sadness. He dropped the football and walked over to me before crouching down to my level.

"Jeremy. Your mum and I... we're not going to get back together. It would be impossible now. And once I've got my new house sorted, we're going to start properly with the divorce proceedings."

I didn't know what *proceedings* meant but it sounded official, it sounded bad.

"Well, when will you get your new house?" I asked, wondering how long I had to change his mind about the whole thing.

"I'm meeting the estate agent next weekend. By this time next week, it should all be sorted. I'm sorry Jeremy, but after that there'll be no turning back. Your mum and I will be getting divorced."

One week? I had just one flimsy week to save their marriage. I needed a way to persuade him.

"But... What if it affects me?" I said weakly. "What if I become a gangster?"

Dad laughed. "A gangster? You? You're a good kid, Jeremy. You'll be fine."

I had to seriously think about a new plan. It was going to take something drastic to change Dad's mind about the divorce.

"There's also something else…" Dad hesitated for a moment. He was obviously trying to choose the right words. "There's something else I need to tell you. When I move into my new house, there's going to be… Well, there's going to be someone else living with me."

Someone else? Why would Dad have someone else living with him? Perhaps he couldn't afford the new place on his own. Maybe he was sharing the cost with a mate.

"Who?" I asked. "One of your friends?"

"Well… Yes. Sort of. We'll talk about it next week. You know, when everything's finalised."

Dad didn't sound very convincing. It made me wonder who'd be living in this new house with him. He obviously didn't want me to know the truth just yet. Why? Was it going to hurt me?

Then a horrifying thought hit me.

Perhaps he was replacing me.

Perhaps he was adopting a new son. A son who was really good at football.

I started to panic. In less than a week, Dad would have a new house, he'd start divorce 'proceedings' and then begin a fresh life with his newly adopted son.

I needed to stop all of this, sharpish!

CHAPTER NINE:
EATING BEETLES

On Monday, life without Miss Hope began. My ankle felt much better now but that was about the only positive of the day.

To say that Mrs Skarratt's classes were like being in Hell would be a bit harsh on Hell — they were much worse.

Mrs Skarratt made us work in silence, and we started the day by listening to her crow-like voice for more than an hour while she went on and on about how children were nothing but germ-carrying weasels.

The work she gave us was too hard for everyone (except Herbert Humphreys — it was still too easy for him) and Mrs Skarratt seemed to take great pleasure in cackling at our answers and calling us stupid.

"If a circle has a radius of 7cm," she said, watching us all with her small piggy eyes, "how could you work out the circumference?"

Alfie Brown put up his hand. "What's a scum fronts?" He meant circumference.

Mrs Skarratt shook her head. "Are you really *that* thick, Brown?"

She called everyone by their surname. Brown, Humphreys, Kumar, McNulty, Letchkov. The only person that she didn't call by his surname was Michael, because she couldn't pronounce it properly. Nkrumah. She just called him Whisper Boy, as she'd given him detention for talking in my ear.

When the bell rang at the end of maths, everybody started tidying our books and equipment away.

"What do you think you're doing?!" she yelled.

"Tidying the class," someone told her.

She hissed like a bus when it pulls up to stop.

"A tidy classroom is a sign of precious time being wasted! From now on, we do less tidying and more hard work!"

Some people thought this was a good thing, but I didn't. Miss Hope (now Mrs Bunyan) had always made us keep the classroom neat and tidy, which gave it a welcoming feeling as soon as you arrived at school.

During English class, we were given the hardest spelling test in history — what the heck is a 'mortgage'? — and then did dictation for an hour. This involved us listening to Mrs Skarratt's vinegary voice read pages and pages from a cookbook called *Catalan Cuisine.* We then had to write down every word she read. We ended up writing an entire recipe for a Catalan Paella. I didn't learn anything, other than the fact that paella is a meal made up of rice and that you shouldn't eat clams that don't open.

I'd never been more relieved to hear the lunchtime bell.

"Whisper Boy and Green," Mrs Skarratt squawked, as we filed out of class. "You two have detention for laughing on Friday. Straight back here as soon as you've eaten your lunch!"

I hate my boring surname. Green. I wished I was called something exciting like Jeremy Jaguar or Jeremy Falcon. Not Green, the colour of spinach and snot. Dad says it's a strong name because it's the colour of money in America. Unfortunately, I lived in England and didn't have a penny to my name.

*

Michael and I ate our lunch slowly, trying to delay our detention with Mrs Skarratt. Luckily, Mum had made ham salad sandwiches for my lunch, so I saved a bit of lettuce and cucumber for Pea and Pod.

"I wonder what Mrs Skarratt has for lunch," said Michael, taking a bite from his turkey twizzler.

I shrugged. "Probably something horrid like beetles or cockroaches or coal."

"I had to eat cockroaches once," said Michael. "When we got stuck on a desert island."

Draining the remains of my *Um Bongo* carton, I ignored Michael's obvious lie and then threw my rubbish in the bin. I stood up, ready to face Mrs Skarratt, and shoved the scraps of salad into my pocket.

A tasty meal that the snails would never get to eat.

Mrs Skarratt was waiting for us in her chair when we returned to class. The room was a bit of a mess with books and stationery scattered across the tables.

"Whisper Boy and Green. Where have you two been? Fifteen minutes to eat your lunch? What are you? Sloths? I ate mine in a hundred and seventy five seconds, just under three minutes. But I guess you two buffoons wouldn't have been able to work that one out."

She showed her teeth like a snarling wolf. There were bits of black food stuck to her gums. Had she *actually* been eating beetles?

Without wasting any time, she told us to sit down on the carpet in front of her. She then began taking off her filthy walking boots. They were caked in mud. I could smell dog poo.

When she tugged them from her feet, she revealed a pair of grubby white socks. Well, I imagined that they used to be white. They were now dark grey and covered in brown and green stains. They clearly hadn't been washed for weeks, if not months!

She was about to hand the boots over when portly Mrs Gillott, the Year 3 teacher, came waddling into the classroom. Mrs Gillott started browsing through one of the bookshelves before she noticed us sitting on the floor in front of Mrs Skarratt.

"Oh, hello," said Mrs Gillott. "What are you lot doing?"

Mrs Skarratt spoke before we had chance to say anything.

"I'm just explaining how to work out the circumference of a circle."

Mrs Gillott arched a quizzical eyebrow. "Circumference of a circle? Is that on the Year 5 curriculum?"

Mrs Skarratt paused for a second, thinking. "No. But it doesn't hurt to stretch their tiny minds, does it?"

I silently prayed that Mrs Gillott would save the day and tell us to go outside. But she didn't.

"I guess not," said Mrs Gillott. "I'm just borrowing this Mental Maths book, okay?"

Mrs Skarratt nodded and then watched Mrs Gillott leave with her narrow, suspicious eyes. As soon as the door was closed, she gave us one boot each.

"By the end of lunchtime, I want to be able to see my face in those shoes."

I looked down at the muddy boot.

"But we don't have anything to clean them with," I said. "How are we meant to make them shine?"

Mrs Skarratt scowled at me. "You have fingers. And you know how to spit, don't you? Now, get on with it."

With that, Mrs Skarratt sat back in her chair, picked up her cookbook – *Catalan Cuisine* – and left us to clean her boots.

After forty minutes of picking at mud, wiping with fingers and spitting on leather, the disgusting boot transformed into something that was reasonably clean. By the end, I felt sick.

"I suppose they'll do," Mrs Skarratt croaked, as we handed the shoes back. "But any more trouble from you two, and you'll be back in here for more of this."

Michael bolted immediately from the room, clearly desperate to get away from Mrs Skarratt and enjoy the last five minutes of lunchtime.

I stood up, stretched my tired arms and then wandered over to the snails' tank. When I got there, I couldn't believe my eyes. The tank was empty! Well, not quite empty. Pea and Pod were still inside but the tank was bare. No soil, no leaves, no empty margarine tubs for them to hide inside. They must have been bored and cold and confused.

I lifted the tank lid and took out the salad leaves from my pocket. But I didn't get to feed them.

"Oi!" Mrs Skarratt barked. "What do you think you're doing, you filthy little urchin?!"

I turned around to face her. She put down her cookbook and trotted her skinny goat-legs over to the tank.

"Where's all the soil?" I asked. "They need some food too."

She brushed past me, the whiff of her dirty coat filling my nostrils. It stunk of horses, petrol and wrongdoing. She slammed the tank lid shut with a BANG. It must have almost deafened the poor snails.

"They've got food," Mrs Skarratt growled. "Look." She pointed to one end of the tank, where I saw some yellow powder scattered. It looked like grated parmesan cheese.

"What's that?" I asked.

"Cornmeal," she said. "Keeps 'em healthy."

"Cornmeal? But they like lettuce and cucumber best." I held up my scraps of salad. Mrs Skarratt immediately ripped the greens from my hand.

"They're on a special new diet. Cornmeal only. Now get out of this class."

I was suddenly hit with a wave of sadness. I wanted to cry and I badly wished that Miss Hope would come back right now.

As I left, I gave Pea and Pod one last glance. They looked sad too in their empty glass tank. In fact, they looked seriously depressed. I just hoped that they wouldn't have the same fate as Fanny.

*

Mum took me to *McDonald's* for tea that night. She ordered a *McChicken Sandwich* for herself while I had a *Happy Meal*. It came with a toy – some weird elephant from a movie that I hadn't seen.

As we tucked into our chips, I tried to tell Mum about my terrible day – that Mrs Skarratt had made me clean her dirty boots. But Mum didn't believe me.

"Is this because of the divorce?" she said, before taking a sip of still *Fanta*. "Do you feel like you need more attention? Is that why you're making these things up?"

I put down my hamburger. "I'm not making it up. It's true."

"Well, who else was there?" she asked.

"Michael."

Mum rolled her eyes. "Okay. Now it all makes sense. You expect me to believe Michael? The boy who once told me that he'd won an Oscar for a film he directed. So, now you two are cooking up fantasy stories about the teacher making you clean her boots. What else did she make you do? Polish the horn on her unicorn's head?"

I decided not to talk about it anymore. Monday had been a terrible day and I'd just have to pretend it never happened. Mum always said that whenever you have a bad day, just screw the memory up in a ball and throw it away, because tomorrow is a new day and great things could happen tomorrow.

This hadn't been working for Mum lately though, because I heard her every night in her room. She would cry for ages before she went to sleep. That's if she even managed any sleep. Some mornings she looked like a zombie, the walking dead.

She missed Dad (obviously) and Fanny (probably). I just wished that she'd let him move back in.

Anyway, I tried to forget about Monday, because tomorrow is a new day. Unfortunately, tomorrow was Tuesday. And Tuesday would make Monday feel like a happy dream.

CHAPTER TEN: TALONS OF A VULTURE

The sun never seemed to rise on Tuesday morning. The sky stayed dark and a fine drizzle whipped through the air, making everything feel damp and miserable.

"It's that wet rain," my gran always used to say, which I never understood. Isn't *all* rain wet? To be honest, Gran never made much sense. Dad said she'd gone completely potty by the time she died. She used to put mustard on her cereal and ate wax crayons as a snack.

Even the snails would know not to eat wax crayons. They mainly eat green vegetables. I wondered if they *would* eat a green wax crayon, if they were desperate, but I don't think they would.

Some people think that snails are insects because they're small and live in the garden, but they're not. Insects must have six legs. Miss Hope taught us that before she deserted us. Snails don't have any legs at all. They're actually gastropods. So are slugs and limpets.

My clothes felt damp by the time I'd walked to school on this particular Tuesday. Pea and Pod looked more depressed than ever in their empty glass prison with nothing to eat but yellow powder. It looked like sawdust. I bet they hated it.

Mrs Skarratt's hair was super greasy, as if she'd been washing her hair in chip fat. And the classroom was still a mess from the previous day, which was starting to make me as depressed as the snails.

Again, skinny Mrs Skarratt started the day by waffling on about how us children were ruining schools around the country and we needed more discipline in our lives. We just sat there in silence, all sitting up straight.

By the time we got on to maths, I'd had enough of the day already. My mind was too occupied, worrying about Dad and Mum and the poor snails.

"So," barked Mrs Skarratt, "if the radius of a circle is 3cm, how would we work out the circumference?" I was staring outside, watching fat blobs of rain running down the window when I suddenly heard my name. "Green! How would you work it out?"

I looked around the room. Everyone else looked just as bored and confused as me.

"I dunno." I shrugged my shoulders. "None of this is on the Year Five curriculum." (I'd heard Mrs Gillot say it yesterday).

In that moment, Mrs Skarratt's sickly pale skin changed to a light pink, then red, then a ferociously dark purple. "GET UP AND COME HERE!" she growled.

I felt a hard lump in my throat as I suddenly became worried. This woman was clearly batty, forcing children to clean her muddy boots. What would she do next?

I stood up and slowly made my way to the front of the class. I could feel every pair of eyes on me.

"Who's in charge in this class?" she hissed, her voice now dangerously soft.

I thought for a second, trying to come up with a funny answer, but my mind went blank.

"You are," I muttered.

"That's right," she said, the mole on her nose twitching like a hairy caterpillar. "So I decide what's on the curriculum. Not you." She stared at me hard for a moment with those cold narrow eyes. "I think you need to show me some respect. And I mean *really* show me some respect. Down on your knees."

This took me by surprise. "Sorry — what?"

"Get down on your knees," she growled.

I did as she said and began to worry what she might do next. I'd seen in books and films that teachers used to hit kids with a cane in Victorian times. It wouldn't surprise me if Mrs Skarratt had a cane in her handbag, right next to her *Catalan Cuisine* cookbook. She looked like she could actually be from the Victorian times. She had wrinkles deeper than those in an elephant's armpit.

Kneeling before her, I started to panic. Was she really going to hit me with a stick?

What *did* happen next came as a total shock. Not one of us could have predicted the next three words that came out of the old hag's mouth.

Mrs Skarratt sat down in her chair while I stayed perfectly still, on my knees in front of her. She bent down and then carefully started removing her boots, extremely muddy once more. She either lived on a farm or crossed a horse's field to get to school.

What was she up to? Did she want me to clean her boots in front of the whole class?

Once the boots were off, she then started to peel away her disgusting socks. This pair were also white but had been stained yellow with sweat.

When the horrid socks came off, I almost threw up because her feet were DISGUSTING! Her toenails were long like the talons of a vulture, only a nasty orange colour and filled with chunks of dirt. They couldn't have been cut for a year!

Her toes were swarming with thick black hairs and between them there were bits of fluff, breadcrumbs and something that looked like a bogie! The bottom of her feet were yellow and covered in verrucas. And on her right foot, standing proud, was a massive wart.

As she wriggled her claw-like toes, an almighty stench hit my nostrils. The filthy feet smelled worse than a cheese shop that only sold out-of-date Stilton.

"Now!" she barked, wiping the greasy fringe from her forehead. "Show me the respect I deserve. Kiss my feet."

I was almost sick right there and then. The old witch was clearly mad! I wanted to tell her to get lost, but thought better of it. It might make things even worse. I glanced around at my classmates. Everyone sat with a terrified look on their face, not daring to move.

"It's no good looking at them, Green," the old hag said. "None of them have been cheeky like you. Just give the feet a quick peck to show me some respect. Otherwise, it's lunchtime detentions for the rest of the month."

I looked down at the hairy feet and I wanted to cry. Why was she doing this to me? If I kissed her feet, I'd be the laughing stock of the school.

But could I really face a whole month of cleaning her boots at lunchtime?

"Come on," she snapped. "We haven't got all day!"

I held my breath, closed my eyes and went for it. I pecked the hard skin on top of her left foot quickly, avoiding the wart completely. The cheesy stink got worse as I did it, and I felt some of her thick hairs press against my lips.

A satisfied smirk slithered across Mrs Skarratt's face.

"That's better," she whispered. "Now, you'll only have detention until the end of the week."

For the rest of the lesson, I could feel her filth on my lips like a disease burning the skin on my face. I wanted to vomit. I wanted to cry. My life had turned into a complete nightmare.

*

As soon as the bell rang, I rushed to the little boys' room and turned on the hot tap. I waited until the water was completely boiling before holding my mouth beneath it. I needed to wash away any traces of the horrid experience I'd just been through.

Once I'd rinsed my lips, I grabbed about thirty paper towels and wiped and wiped and wiped at my face.

And yet, I still felt dirty.

I went to my school bag and grabbed my playtime snack, a small pot of *Hartley's Blackcurrant Jelly*. Mum had packed a spoon for me too.

When I eventually went outside to play, I could feel everyone's eyes on me. People were whispering and pointing.

Did they all know what had happened with Mrs Skarratt? It even felt like the teachers were laughing at me.

The damp drizzle continued to swarm through the playground, wetting everything in its path. I peeled off the lid of my jelly pot and threw it in one of the school litter bins, which are all shaped like frogs (for some reason). You put the litter into the frog's mouth. I don't know why the bins were frogs. I guess that litter attracts flies, and frogs eat flies. That's all I could think of.

After a couple of minutes – eating my jelly by the bin – one of the small kids from the year below came up to me with his friends.

"Is it true?" he said, giggling. "Did you *really* kiss your teacher's feet?" All of the little gang then howled with laughter. I could feel my face turning red.

I heard a couple of older girls making up a song.

"Jeremy Green. Kissed a foot. Best be careful or he'll kiss your butt!"

They shrieked with laughter before starting the verse again. This time, some other girls joined in too. Embarrassing. As more and more people crowded around, it felt like the whole school was laughing at me. My eyes began to fill with tears.

I tried to carry on eating my jelly. I scooped some up onto the spoon, and was about to put it in my mouth when I heard something that stopped me.

"Jeremy's got Skarratt disease!" someone shouted. "Don't let him touch you!"

After a collective intake of breath, the crowd took a step back, away from me — the boy poisoned by Mrs Skarratt's filthy witch germs. The older girls started their chant once more, adding new lines to it this time.

"Jeremy Green. Licked a toe. He liked the taste so he had another go!"

The jelly on my spoon wobbled like mad as my hand started to shake. Why was this happening? Feeling annoyed, I threw my jelly in the bin (along with Mum's spoon). I didn't want to listen to their taunts any more so I charged away from the crowd. Everyone moved out of my way, not wanting to be infected with Skarratt virus.

Away from the pack, I raced over to the opposite side of school and sat down on a wet bench near the sports field. The damp wood immediately soaked through my trousers and wet my bum but I didn't care. I just wanted to be away from everyone's jeers.

Everyone left me alone for the rest of playtime. Some came to point and laugh but nobody wanted to be too close. I was infected now. My cousin, Floyd, asked if I was alright but I told him to go away.

As I brooded over the way my life had fallen apart over the last couple of weeks, I felt a dark gloom cloud my mind and a crack run through my heart. I wished I could go back to being nine again. If this was what things were like as a ten-year-old, I never wanted to be eleven.

After a while on my own, Michael eventually came to sit next to me. I looked at him but didn't say anything. He smiled, gave me a 'hello' nod and sat down on the wet bench.

We sat there in silence for a while. My mind ticked away like a furious clock. I began biting my nails as I seethed over everything that had happened. Mum and Dad's divorce. Miss Hope leaving us. Fanny's death. PC Jade Jackson following me like a bad smell. The snails. The poor snails, being starved by that nasty old witch. And now — also thanks to her — I was the laughing stock of the school.

I felt like a boiling kettle. Angry steam was building inside me. And it felt like the rage wasn't going to stop. It felt like one more thing – just one tiny annoyance – could cause me to erupt like a volcano in school uniform.

"I had to kiss a camel's foot to save my life once," said Michael.

And there it was.

I couldn't stop myself. The kettle of fury had finally hit boiling.

"No you didn't!" I screamed in a voice that didn't sound like my own. "You've never kissed a camel's foot! You've never had to save your own life! You just make things up all the time, Michael."

My mind quickly threw up some of the stories he'd told me in the past. I stood up as the anger continued to build.

"You never won that karate competition in Japan. You were never asked by NASA to test out their new rockets. You never broke into the Houses of Parliament to see what sort of cheese they had in the fridge. And you never caught a killer whale when you fished in the Thames last year! You're a fake, a phony, a fraud. Nothing you ever say is true! I can't believe I even hang around with you."

I thought about how my detentions with Mrs Skarratt had first come about — Michael whispering in my ear. A few days later and I'm the biggest joke in the school. And wasn't it Michael's idea to break into the pet shop? Now I've got the police watching my every move.

"This is all your fault! You're always getting me in trouble."

Michael just sat on the bench, silently looking at me. Then I remembered a word that Dad had used.

"You're nothing but a waster."

At that, Michael stood up. I could see that his eyes were filling with tears. His bottom lip started to shake. He opened his mouth to say something, but then stopped and ran off, leaving me alone once again.

On the other side the playground, one of the teachers blew her whistle for the end of playtime and everyone started making their way inside. I just stood there for a moment, breathing heavily in the rain. As the furious energy quickly drained from my body, I suddenly felt very alone.

CHAPTER ELEVEN:
THE PURGE

Michael didn't speak to me for the rest of the day. He didn't
even look at me. Wednesday morning was the same too. It felt
like our friendship was finished. Not that I really cared. The
only thing that mattered to me at that moment was getting my
parents back together. And Michael couldn't help me with that.

At lunchtime on Wednesday, I was cleaning Mrs Skarratt's
boots again. I'd become used to it by now and had worked out
the best ways to piggle mud out of the hardest crevices. I also
snuck in a few paper towels from the toilet. I used those on any
bits that smelled like horse manure.

Cleaning the boots gave me chance to think of ways to help
Dad move back home. I thought of doing something really
romantic like cooking Mum's favourite Chinese meal and
pretending that Dad had done it. But then I remembered that I
didn't know how to cook.

Mrs Skarratt obviously did. Every lunchtime, as I scrubbed and spit-polished her boots, she always sat in her chair, reading her cookbook. *Catalan Cuisine.* I often wondered what was so interesting about it. Why would anyone want to read a cookbook? They were the most boring sorts of books in the world. I liked exciting books where pirates hunt for gold or teenagers creep through haunted houses or explorers escape from vicious monsters. Cookbooks were about as exciting as queueing in the post office.

After wondering about Mrs Skarratt's book for so long, I realised that I hadn't had any good ideas about Mum and Dad. But then, at precisely 12:43 (I checked on my Casio watch), an intriguing opportunity arose.

I looked up to see Mrs Skarratt put down the book on *Catalan Cuisine.* She scratched the hairy mole on the side of her nose and then poked her bony finger inside the nose for a vigorous root around. I saw her pull out some green treasure and wipe it on her filthy handkerchief. After that, the skinny old witch stood up, pulled the skirt out of her bottom and ambled out of the room.

Mrs Skarratt had left the cookbook on her desk. I had to know what was inside.

Through the classroom window, I watched Mrs Skarratt. Like a hunchback goat, she trotted off in the direction of our headteacher Miss Frearson's office. The staff toilets were right next to this, so I guessed that's where she was going. This would give me a few minutes.

Leaving the boots on the floor, I jumped to my feet and rushed over to the desk. I had one last check that nobody was watching before opening the cookbook.

At first, I was bitterly disappointed. I looked carefully at the first few pages. It was just like any other recipe book. A map at the start showed that Catalonia is in the north of Spain, and borders France. Then it went straight into the recipes. Paellas, stews, weird looking mushroom dishes. It was just a normal cookbook. I'd seen black and white snooker videos that were more exciting.

Then, as I flicked through, the book suddenly opened on a page that had been folded at the corners. Some of the sentences had been underlined in pencil. It seemed like Mrs Skarratt had been paying particular attention to this recipe.

I looked at the photo on the page but couldn't quite work out was the food was meant to be. It looked like some sort of stew. Then, I looked up at the page title and my heart skipped six beats.

Escargots Catalans *(Catalan-Style Snails)*

1. **Collect your snails.** You can find snails on potted plants or in the garden. They tend to like lettuce, kale, cabbage, and strawberries. Just pull them off and put them in a basket or bowl.

2. **Wash your snails.** Since snails crawl around in dirt, you need to make sure they are really clean. Rinse them in a colander under cold running water while rubbing them together.

3. **Purge the snails.** Controlled feeding of snails ensures they are clean of diseases, toxins and dirt. Put

the snails into an empty tank with only yellow cornmeal to eat. Do this for about a week. You'll know the purge is working when you see yellow and green poo trails in the tank.

4. **Salt the snails.** Put the snails in a small bowl and sprinkle them with the 2 tablespoons salt. This kills them. Fill the bowl with water and then drain. Repeat as needed, rinsing off the salt and mucus each time, until the water runs clear. Now your snails are ready to cook.

My heart was hammering like a horse's hoof on concrete. I dropped the cookbook on the floor and rushed over to the snail tank. Inside, I saw something that made my stomach flip with fear.

Green and yellow poo trails.

This was part of the 'purge' process. Mrs Skarratt was feeding them cornmeal to get rid of any toxins. The book said that this had to go on for a week. When had it started? Yesterday? Mrs Skarratt was planning to eat Pea and Pod next Monday! I had to get them out of there.

I had just started to lift the lid off the tank when I heard her bitter, oniony voice outside the class.

"Oi," she screeched at someone in the corridor. "Stop smiling! You're at school, not Disneyland."

Then I heard her marching towards the door. I didn't have time to save the snails now. Quickly and quietly, I put down the lid and darted back to the carpet. I was about to carry on cleaning the boots when I noticed the cookbook in the middle of the floor where I'd dropped it. Skarratt's footsteps came closer. I rolled across the floor, grabbed the book and leapt over to place it on her desk. The door handle turned and the door began to open. I dived to the ground, landing on the boots, just as the old goat burst into the room. She eyed me suspiciously, like an old pirate who thought I was going to steal her treasure.

"What you up to, you filthy little blister?" she growled.

I shook my head and tried to wipe the guilty look off my face. "Nothing."

Her eyes narrowed and she licked her dry lips with her lizard-like tongue.

"Right," she said. "Out you go then. Get the last five minutes of play."

I rushed out of the classroom and grabbed my coat. Outside, the weather was grey and miserable again, just like my mood. A light rain still filled the air. I wanted to tell somebody about the snails but I knew nobody would listen — I was still infected with Skarratt disease.

And then I saw Michael.

He was playing football with some older lads when I grabbed him by the arm.

"Michael. Mrs Skarratt is planning to kill the snails and —"

Michael batted my arm away, which stopped me talking.

"What do you think you're doing?" he said.

I sensed other people listening so I lowered my voice.

"Mrs Skarratt is going to kill the snails and —"

"You're unbelievable, Jeremy," he said, stepping away from me. "You come talking to me about snails when you haven't even apologised for the nasty things you said to me yesterday."

"Yeah, of course I'm sorry. But we need to save the snails." I moved closer to him so that I could speak in a lower voice but Michael pushed me in the chest.

"We're not friends anymore," he yelled with a thunderous look on his face.

Before I knew it, we were suddenly surrounded by a small crowd.

"Punch him!" someone shouted.

"Smack him, Mike!"

"Do us a favour. He's diseased."

The crowd quickly grew bigger and a chant started.

"FIGHT! FIGHT! FIGHT!"

I felt someone push me in the back and I stumbled forwards, right into Michael's personal space. He reacted quickly and punched me right in the nose. I felt the dull thud before I realised what had happened. My eyes immediately started to water. I don't think I was crying but my eyes filled up at the pain. The punch sent me staggering backwards before one of the crowd pushed me again. This time, I lost my balance and fell down, scraping my knee as I hit the floor.

Above me, I then heard a dinner lady's whistle, blowing like mad. I looked up to see the crowd parting. Some of the older boys put their arms around Michael and patted him on the back. They were laughing and cheering, like Romans leaving the Colosseum, happy with their lunchtime entertainment (we did Romans last year).

I touched my nose. It killed. When I looked down at my fingers, I saw they had blood on them. I needed to go and wash my nose in the toilets.

Just before I got to my feet, Michael glanced round at me.

He wasn't laughing.

He wasn't cheering.

In fact, I think I saw a tear running down his cheek.

CHAPTER TWELVE:
MRS GILLESPIE'S MISTAKE

I wrote a letter to our headteacher, Miss Frearson, but I crossed loads of it out because I didn't want her to know that I'd written it. Miss Frearson had a temper shorter than one of Snow White's seven friends. She could make the toughest kids cry with just a few seconds of her steely glare. We'd nicknamed her Miss Fearsome.

Dear Miss ~~Fearsome~~ Frearson,

~~This is Jeremy Green.~~ ~~This is a Year 5 student.~~ This is an angry animal lover. I have top-secret information about your disgusting new teacher, Mrs Skarratt.

~~During my detention on Wednesday, I looked in her cookbook.~~

Mrs Skarratt is nothing but a stinky old piece of haggis and she is planning to KILL AND EAT ~~our~~ her class's pet snails. Please look in her cookbook. It is called Catalan Cuisine. There is a page about eating snails.

She has already started purging ~~my good friends~~ Pea and Pod, and will eat them for tea on Monday evening. If you don't believe me, look at the cornmeal in their tank.

Please save the snails and stop her from this horrible crime.

~~Lots of love~~ from

~~Jeremy Green~~ ~~A Year 5 student.~~

An angry animal lover.

P.S. Mrs Skarratt makes ~~me~~ some children pick poo and mud off her boots at lunchtime.

P.P.S. Mrs Skarratt also made ~~me~~ a child kiss
her disgusting feet. She is a nasty, cruel old hag.
P.P.P.S. Can you please sack her?

After I'd finished writing the letter, I wasn't sure what to do with it. Even though Mrs Skarratt was horrible, I was also scared of Miss Fearsome. What if she found out that I'd sent the letter? What if Mrs Skarratt and Miss Fearsome were best friends and were planning to eat the snails together? What if this letter got me into even more trouble than I was already in?

I folded the letter up and put it in my pocket.

*

After school I decided to walk around town. I wasn't going anywhere in particular but I didn't want to be at home. It didn't even feel like home any more, not without Dad or Fanny. Plus, I felt like the fresh air would clear my mind.

I had two major issues to deal with and not a lot of time to deal with them. Somehow I had to save my parents' marriage before the weekend when Dad would buy his new house. I also needed to save Pea and Pod before next Monday when Mrs Skarratt will have successfully 'purged' them, ready to eat. It felt like the Countdown clock was ticking away on my life, faster and louder than ever.

Mum wasn't going to help me. Miss Hope had deserted me. Michael hated me.

I was truly on my own.

As I wandered aimlessly through the town centre, the rain continued to fall and I kept my hood tight over my head. Then I passed a gift store. It wasn't usually the sort of shop that I would ever pay attention to, but on this occasion, something caught my eye.

In the window display, there were all sorts of naff gifts that mums and grandmas were interested in. Flowery handbags, flowery teapots, flowery lampshades, flowery chairs, flowery suitcases, flowery dresses, flowery flowerpots, flowery flowers. Basically, flowery everything. The display was given a cutesy-wutesy village fete impression with some flowery bunting hanging above. Like I said, this sort of thing never usually appealed to me. But…

It was in this window that I saw it.

Hanging on the back of a flowery chair was a tea towel. Around the edge of the tea towel were pictures of animals. A cat, a dog, a rabbit, a goldfish. Hamsters, guinea pigs, mice. And in the centre were seven words that seemed to shine from the shadows

A FAMILY ISN'T COMPLETE WITHOUT A PET!

In that instant, I knew precisely how to solve my problems. I knew precisely how to achieve *both* my goals in one brilliant swoop. I knew precisely how to kill two birds with one stone… Actually, I didn't like that saying. In fact, I would be doing the complete opposite to killing anything.

*

Thursday was just as bad as the rest of the week. Wet weather, horrible lessons, lunchtime detention cleaning muddy boots. The snail tank was still depressingly bare and there were more of the green and yellow droppings.

Michael didn't speak to me all day, nor did anyone else really. Leah Ford asked to borrow my rubber in maths but that was about it.

Anyway, the part of Thursday that was most interesting came after school. My plan — in case you hadn't worked it out already — was to steal the snails from school and take them home. Not only would this save them from being eaten by evil Mrs Skarratt, it would also give our house a new pet, which would hopefully bring Mum and Dad back together again.

The biggest problem was that I couldn't take them during school time because Mrs Skarratt watched the snails like a hawk. The only time she left them alone was when she went to the toilet, and she'd notice immediately if they were gone. As I was the only person who paid them any attention, she would have known I'd taken them.

So I planned to steal them long after school had finished. The Great Snail Robbery would take place on Friday night. But first I had some investigating to do.

*

The plan was simple. Break into school (without doing any damage), grab the snails and take them home to fill Mum's heart with kindness and love — just like Miss Hope had once said.

There were just a few things standing in my way. Firstly, there was the alarm system. Each room and corridor had a sensor in the corner. I watched the sensor in our class on Thursday. It glowed with a red light for precisely four seconds. Then the light went out for four seconds. Then back on again. The sensors were the same in every room.

I knew that during the day the sensors weren't active. But once everybody left for the night, our caretaker, Mrs Gillespie, would lock up and set the alarm. When the alarm was set, any movements below the sensors would set off the sirens.

Before I even considered the alarms though, I would actually need to get into the building. So, after I'd eaten my tea on Thursday evening — a pork dinner with peas, carrots, broccoli and gravy — I went back to school to do a stakeout.

*

Our school was pretty modern, not like one of those old-fashioned Hogwarts sorts of school. Ours was all built on one level. No stairs or anything to worry about. And the metal fencing that ran around the school was all pretty close to the building. This meant that I could get a good look at the way Mrs Gillespie locked up at night.

As I took my place next to the school fence near the playground, I noticed that a couple of windows were still open. They were the sorts of windows that slid from side to side.

According to my Casio watch, it was 17:41 when I saw Mrs Gillespie checking the windows. 17:41 actually means 5:41pm, which actually means nineteen minutes to six. I've always been pretty good at telling the time.

Mrs Gillespie was a large lady with short purple hair (dyed, obviously) and a permanently red face. Her breath smelled of fags and Mum said she goes to the pub every day. I can't blame her though. I bet she needs to relax after doing her job. It must be pretty stressful having to lock up an entire school.

Everyone thinks that the teachers are the cleverest people at our school, but I think it's Mrs Gillespie. She can do just about anything. I'd seen her fix all sorts of things; toilets, bikes, holes in the walls. I'd seen her put up fences, chop down trees, paint the white football pitch on our school field. She knew exactly what sort of chemicals would clean different kinds of stains; blackcurrant juice, vomit, the dog muck that Kyle McNulty trampled in on his shoes. She was unbelievably clever.

From the fence, I watched Mrs Gillespie move to one of the open windows. She slid it shut, locked it and then disappeared from the room. Moments later, she was in the next class — our class. She checked that the windows were all locked and then moved on. As she went around the school locking windows, I followed her around the fence. I could easily make out her purple hair.

It seemed like she did a pretty thorough job of checking and locking the windows, and I was beginning to wonder how I could possibly get inside when I noticed she made a mistake.

Mrs Gillespie checked every single window… apart from one. From what I could tell, the only window she didn't bother with was the one next to the staff toilet, right near Miss Fearsome's office. I guessed that nobody ever opened it, which was why the caretaker never checked it. Luckily though, Mrs Gillespie's mistake gave me a way in.

CHAPTER THIRTEEN: REAL SECRET AGENT

When I got to school on Friday, I wanted to tell Michael about my plan. He would have loved it. But I couldn't risk another punch in the face. My nose was still throbbing from the previous day.

The weather had stayed gloomy and wet on Friday. I got to school early and went straight to the reception desk near the school offices. I asked the office manager, Mrs Dunhill, about the price of school dinners, but I couldn't have cared less about them really. I was only *actually* interested in one thing... getting a look at the corridor near the Miss Fearsome's office. I could see the window at the end — the one that Mrs Gillespie didn't check. Above it, I saw an alarm sensor and below it, a table. This gave me an idea.

I felt like a real secret agent as I started to plan my route.

After entering through *that* window, I would come up past the headteacher's office and then turn left into the corridor that led to our class. There was one motion sensor in that corridor and one more in class. That made three sensors in total.

As well as the sensors, there was also another problem. Last night, after I'd watched Mrs Gillespie set the alarms and lock up, she'd also locked the big metal gates at the school entrance. These gates, along with the fence that ran around the perimeter, had sharp spikes at the top of them, so there was no way I could scale them.

I'd had to come up with a new idea. So, at playtime, I went into the nursery class and made conversation with one of the teachers, Mrs Ferguson. We had a pointless two-minute chit-chat about the amount of glitter on the floor, how crisp packets sometimes have hardly any crisps in them and the reasons why the glue sticks' lids go missing.

After we'd finished, Mrs Ferguson failed to notice me walk off with one of the plastic spades from the nursery play area.

I took the spade into the playground and over to the school field. A light rain was spitting through the air, enough to keep the grass soggy. After checking that nobody was watching me, I sprinted across the wet grass to the opposite side of the field. I pressed my foot into the soft ground. It made a super-squelchy sound, so I started to dig. If I couldn't get over the fence, I would go under.

*

The blue post-it notes on Mrs Skarratt's desk were going to be very important to my mission. In case you didn't know, post-it notes are little squares of coloured paper with a sticky bit at the top. You could write notes on them and then stick them to things. I've seen teachers do it loads.

I'd spotted the ones on Mrs Skarratt's desk during maths on Friday morning. They may have only been paper, but today they shone to me like sparkling sapphires among Mrs Skarratt's scrunched-up paperwork and dirty coffee cups.

For the first time in ages, I rushed my lunch on Friday and almost sprinted to my boot-cleaning detention. Not that I wanted to clean the boots, or be anywhere near that filthy fleabag, Mrs Skarratt. But if she left the room, I wanted to be there.

When I walked into class, the old witch was sitting in her chair, picking at a spot on her chin with grubby fingers. Her boots were already off — as dirty as a sheep's backside — and her cookbook was in her hand.

She didn't look at me when I entered, she just grunted like a sick crow. I grabbed one of the boots and got on with the job.

It wasn't until 12:47 (according to my Casio) that she left the room in the direction of the staff toilet. And then I sprang into action.

I jumped to my feet and darted to the teacher's desk for the thick pad of blue post-it notes. I pulled four of them off — one for each sensor and a spare one (just in case). I ran over to the corner of the room where the sensor's red light slowly flashed on and off. Grabbing the nearest chair, I pulled it into the corner and stood on it. I reached up, stretching my arms as high as they'd go. I felt as tall as a giraffe. I peeled off the top post-it note and carefully stuck it onto the sensor, making sure that all of the red light was covered. Happy with my work, I jumped down to the carpet, put the chair in its place and rushed back to the boots, just as Mrs Skarratt came trotting down the hallway.

At afternoon break, I retrieved the plastic spade I'd hidden in a box of musical instruments (nobody ever used them) and then stealthily returned to the school field to find my hole by the fence. By the end of playtime, the hole looked big enough to fit a football through it… I just hoped it would fit a ten-year-old boy through.

Once the bell had rung for the end of the day, I hung back and waited for Mrs Skarratt to leave the room. As soon as she did, I grabbed a chair and took it out of class. I wandered along the corridor with it so casually that nobody seemed to take any notice of me. I made sure that nobody was around and acted fast. Just like before, I stood on the chair and pressed the post-it note over the red sensor before jumping down.

That was two out of three sensors covered. Just one more to go.

The final motion sensor could have proved a bit trickier. It was down the corridor that led to the teachers' toilets, past Miss Fearsome's office. Luckily though, there was already a table below it, so I didn't need to take a chair to climb on.

Crouching along the corridor, I felt like an SAS soldier and decided to drop in an army roll as I passed Miss Fearsome's office. I tucked myself under the table beneath the window, taking a moment to assess the situation. I couldn't hear anyone using the staff toilet. In fact, the only sound I could hear was the tap-tapping of our headteacher's computer keyboard.

Miss Fearsome only ever came out of her office for assemblies and to tell off the naughtiest kids. She had short brown hair, a husky cigarette-smoker's voice and wore large-framed spectacles that were tinted brown. She reminded me more of a Bond villain than a headteacher. She once shouted at a boy with such a roar that he wet his pants. The last thing I wanted was to get caught messing around outside her office.

Hidden beneath the table, I felt as invisible as a ninja. I spent a moment in the quiet, taking in my surroundings. Up on the corridor walls were two maps. One of the world and one of the London Underground. I had a similar map of the underground in a book at home. I loved reading the names of London tube stations. Here are some of my favourites:

-   **Brockley** because it sounds like broccoli and that's my favourite vegetable.

- **Mudchute** because it makes me think of sliding down a mud chute, a massive muddy slide, in just my swimming trunks, getting ditched.

- **Swiss Cottage** because it reminds me of a cute, cosy log cabin where you can eat lots of cheese.

- **Golders Green**, **Bethnall Green** and all the other stations with my surname in, even **Greenwich** (which is actually pronounced *Gren-itch).*

- **Piccadilly Circus** is the most fun to say and it has the word circus in it.

- **Elephant and Castle** is probably my favourite because it has an elephant and a castle. What more could you want?

Anyway, after looking up at the maps for a moment, I got on with my mission. Out of my pocket, I pulled out a thick piece of card and the last two post-it notes. There was also something else in the bottom of my pocket… my letter to Miss Fearsome. I'd completely forgotten about it. I placed them all on the carpet in front of me.

First, I grabbed the post-its. Then, like a silent squirrel, I climbed on top of the table and pressed the piece of blue paper over the red sensor before whipping back into my hiding spot.

I waited a moment. My heart was beating like crazy but I managed to keep my breathing on mute. The only sound I could hear was the tap-tap-tapping of Miss Fearsome's keyboard.

Next, I picked up the piece of thick card. I'd found it in one of Mum's drawers last night. The card idea came to me after watching the way that Mrs Gillespie slid the windows shut.

I held my breath a bit longer, listening for anyone coming. When all felt safe, I hopped back onto the table. I pressed the lock and then carefully slid the window to the left. It only opened slightly (to stop any of the teachers escaping) but it was enough. I placed my card in the open gap and then slid the window back to the right. Normally, when the windows close and lock, the lock catches, making a clicking sound. But with my card in the way, this window didn't click.

I shuffled back on my bottom and looked at the window. It looked shut. To anyone who gave it a quick glance, it looked locked. But, thanks to my card, it wasn't quite shut properly. It wasn't locked.

I was just nodding to myself, admiring my work, when I suddenly realised something odd. The corridor had become deathly silent. The tap-tap-tapping sound from Miss Fearsome's keyboard had stopped. I turned around to look at her office. Then I heard footsteps coming towards the door. The door handle started to turn. I didn't have time to get back beneath the table and it might have been too risky anyway. If she caught me snooping around outside her office, I'd be as dead as a dinosaur.

So, as the door began to open, I did the only thing I could possibly do. I slid off the table and barged my way through the nearest door… the women's toilets.

At a glance, the women's toilets seemed a lot nicer than any men's room I'd been in. Above the sink was a mirror and a flower in a glass. The room smelled of sweet perfume and sickly air-freshener, rather than what most little boys' rooms smelled like… strong bleach and stale pee.

I didn't have long to admire the room because I could hear Miss Fearsome's footsteps getting closer. There was only one place to hide. I darted into the toilet cubicle and turned the lock, just as I heard the toilet door creak open.

Miss Fearsome, spoke in her croaky, smoker's voice.

"Oh, there's someone in here. Is that you Rosie?"

Rosie was the portly Year 3 teacher, Mrs Gillott. I'd heard the other teachers call it her. But what was I meant to do? I couldn't talk anything like a teacher!

I tried to say yes, without actually speaking.

"Uh-hmmmm," I muttered, attempting a high pitch.

I heard Miss Fearsome sigh. There was a moment of silence before she then said something that I never expected.

"You still got the runs? Maybe you should get some tablets from the pharmacy. Mrs Skarratt's had the trots all week too. Must be something going round."

I couldn't believe what I was hearing! I wanted to delete the conversation from my head but I couldn't. The horrid images were swimming around in my brain. Surely teachers don't talk about this sort of stuff… do they?!

"Anyway," said Miss Fearsome. "I'll leave you to it."

With that, she left the toilets. I may have only been pretending to be poorly a moment ago, but now I felt properly ill. Once I'd pushed the horrible images out of my mind — of Mrs Gillott and Mrs Skarratt on the toilet — I eventually dared to make my way out of the cubicle. I opened the bathroom door and heard the click-click-clicking of Miss Fearsome's keyboard once more. Not wanting to risk that she might stop, I darted along the corridor, back up to class to collect my belongings and then out of school.

I never realised that I'd left my letter to Miss Fearsome on the floor beneath the table.

CHAPTER FOURTEEN:
LITTLE YELLOW RIDING HOOD

According to this film I saw once, the key to robbing a bank was doing your research. I guess you could say the same about robbing snails from a primary school. So far, I had most things sorted.

- I'd covered the alarm sensors with blue post-it notes.
- I'd dug a football-sized hole under the school fence.
- I'd wedged a piece of card into one of the windows, stopping it from locking

There was just one more thing I needed to do. Near the school window that I was going to climb in through was a CCTV camera. This meant I needed to cover my face. So I headed to the local costume shop, **Fancy Pants**.

I'd found a bit of money in one of my coat pockets (I love it when that happens!). Not quite enough to buy a new pet but hopefully I'd be able to afford a plastic mask.

A buzzer sounded as I opened the shop door and a man behind the counter looked up, observing me through thick glasses. I nodded. He nodded back and then carried on looking at his magazine.

The shop smelled like a second-hand store, a bit like an old-people's home. It was filled with whacky, wonderful outfits. You could dress as Superman, Red Riding Hood, a zombie version of Red Riding Hood, a pirate, a pencil, a pint of beer. There were costumes for babies, costumes for kids, costumes for men and costumes for women. But, as I quickly realised, the only thing they didn't have was the one thing I needed.

The man behind the counter had unwashed, shoulder-length hair and red, spotty skin. He may have only been young but his thick specs and nasally voice made him seem much older.

"Can I help you?" he asked as I approached the counter.

"Erm… do you have any masks?" I asked.

Nasally Man thought for a moment and then shook his head.

"We normally order the masks in just before October. For Halloween. You kids are always changing your minds about what's cool. If we ordered a load of cartoon character masks in now, they'd be out of fashion by October."

Defeated, I made my way back to the door before his nasally voice stopped me.

"Oh, we do have *these* masks," he said, bending down behind the counter. I turned around and excitedly rushed back to the till. Nasally Man placed a cardboard box on the counter with a thud. When he opened the box, my heart sank.

"I guess they're not really your sort of thing," he said.

I sighed. "Not really… but… I'll take one."

Nasally Man looked surprised but didn't hesitate to take my last few pounds from me. And I walked out of **Fancy Pants** with a mask that no hardened criminal would ever be seen wearing.

*

"I'm going to bed," I told Mum, not long after we'd had tea. "Want to be up early for Dad in the morning."

Mum frowned with surprise as I went upstairs and brushed my teeth. In my bedroom, I did ten press-ups to make sure I was completely fit and strong for the mission ahead. Then I turned off the light and climbed into bed.

About ten minutes later, Mum crept into my room, creaking over the floorboards like a monster in a horror movie. I lay there with my eyes closed, as still as a rock, pretending to be asleep. She bent over, kissed me softly on the forehead and then left the room.

Once I'd heard her footsteps going back downstairs, I jumped out of bed and stuffed one of my old cuddly toys under the duvet. Ernie the Orangutan was almost as big as me so I stretched him out where I would have been lying.

After that, I put on my yellow hoodie and climbed out of my bedroom window. I shuffled carefully along the window sill, down the drainpipe and onto Mrs Patel's fence next door. Thankfully, I had better luck than Fanny and made it down unscathed.

*

It felt so weird to be out alone at night. I felt free but also vulnerable, like a chicken who'd escaped the slaughterhouse, only to be surrounded by foxes.

Beneath the moonlight, I kept moving and before I knew it, I was at the school fence. Before I got too close to school and the CCTV cameras, I needed to cover myself up. I pulled the yellow hood over my head and put on the mask I'd bought from **Fancy Pants** costume store earlier. Now, anyone who saw the video recording wouldn't see Jeremy Green breaking into school… they'd see Dora the Explorer.

I found the hole I'd dug and was about to squeeze myself through it when I heard footsteps coming down the path.

With the orange glow of a lamp post behind him, the silhouette of a dark figure approached. My heart was beating so hard, it was practically shaking my entire body. I didn't know what to do.

Should I run?

Should I try to squeeze through the hole?

Should I keep the Dora mask on?

In fact, I spent so long wondering how to act that I just stood there like a stupid deer in the headlights.

The dark figure gradually got closer, and as the glow from another lamp post lit up his face, I realised it was someone I'd met before.

The man had a bushy, white beard that had invaded his entire face but he was completely bald, like he'd put his head on upside-down. Except, tonight in the drizzle, Mr Singh was wearing a sky blue anorak, covered with whales, boats and anchors.

I heard him chuckling as he approached. He stopped in front of me, looking at my face. I could only peek through the tiny holes in the Dora mask.

"That's an interesting mask," he said cheerfully, as if he'd just bumped into his best friend. "You know what they say about people in masks, don't you? They're two-faced! Geddit?"

He giggled to himself for a moment.

"What are you supposed to be?" he asked. "Little Yellow Riding Hood?" Another chuckle.

I nodded slowly. "Erm... Trick or Treat?" My voice came out weird from behind the Dora mask, so I doubt anyone could've guessed it was me.

"Trick or Treat?" Mr Singh laughed. "It's not Halloween yet!"

"Errr... No..." I had to think on my feet. "But it is in Australia."

"Is it?" Mr Singh arched an eyebrow.

"Yes," I said. "Everything's backwards there. They have summer in our winter. When they flush their toilets, the water spins the opposite way around. And they, erm, eat didgeridoos on Christmas Day."

"And they have Halloween in April?" asked Mr Singh.

I nodded. "Yes. Everyone knows that."

Mr Singh chuckled. "Well, you learn something new every day!"

With that, he reached into his pocket and gave me a Werther's Original. He wished me a Happy Halloween and then carried on his way.

Leaving me alone once again, ready to get on with my mission.

Wet ground squelched against my bottom as I squeezed through my mini tunnel. The gap between the fence and the ground was tight but I managed to wriggle through, scraping my nose on the bottom of the fence.

Now, I had the school field ahead of me. I crept across the grass and onto the playground, making my way around to the window that I'd put the piece of card in earlier.

My face had already become sweaty inside the plastic mask. It made my breathing sound like Darth Vader from the Star Wars films. My heart was hammering in my chest and I felt sick with nerves. Still, I knew that I had to do this… to save Pea and Pod's from being killed, and hopefully get my Mum and Dad back together.

But then, I realised something terrible had happened.

*

As I approached the window, my knees almost gave way and my breathing became tight. I couldn't believe what I was seeing… the piece of card had gone.

The window was locked.

No, no, no, no no. No! No! **NO!**

This couldn't be happening.

All of the planning and preparation I'd gone through.

Why?

Why would Mrs Gillespie have checked the window tonight of all nights?

My breath became fast, heavy and hot inside the Dora mask. I wanted to rip it off and throw it away but I knew I'd be on camera right now.

I felt like the world was caving in around me. The damp April air was squeezing me tight, crushing my soul. Everything in my life had fallen to pieces. And the one glimmer of hope — the one thing that I felt could save my happiness — had been snatched away from me.

A tear ran down my cheek and a huge lump had grown in my throat. My hands started to shake as I tried to hold in a scream of anger, a scream of sadness, the scream of my emptying life.

All of a sudden, everything just built up inside me. I felt like a stick of dynamite. My fuse had been lit when Fanny died and had now burnt away… there was nothing left… nothing apart from… BOOM!

It was as if another force had taken control of my body. It didn't feel like I was making my own decisions any more. Things were just happening. Everything was a blur.

I couldn't let the snails die. I couldn't let my parents split up.

I had to break into that school.

I went round to the front entrance and suddenly became convinced that I was a superhuman strongman or an invincible policeman. I charged at the door with all my might and…

I bounced back off it and fell over backwards, landing in a puddle next to an empty pot of Dairylea Dunkers.

Breaking down the door wasn't going to work. Instead, I scrambled around beneath the school minibus and eventually found a huge, sharp rock. Back at the window-that-should-have-been-open, I pulled back my arm — the heavy rock nearly tipping me over — before launching it at the window with enormous effort.

CRASH!!!

I'd actually expected the rock to come bouncing back off the window like I had off the front door. But it didn't. It shattered the glass into millions of tiny shards.

I'd expected the shrill sound of an alarm to pierce the air. But it didn't. The only sound I could hear was the echo of exploding glass.

*

I expected to hear someone running in my direction from a nearby street, shouting at me to stop.

But nobody came.

As I stood there in the deafening silence, I could feel the erratic clippety-clop of my heart. And then I realised two things. Firstly, I had seriously broken the law.

TRESPASSING.

VANDALISM.

BREAKING AND ENTERING.

That's how PC Jade Jackson would put it — along with a load more hideous crimes — as she wrenched the handcuffs onto my wrists.

But secondly, I realised something else… I had a way in. I could save Pea and Pod.

Climbing into school carefully, making sure I didn't cut my hands on any smashed glass, I went in through the window and onto the table on the other side of the window. I leapt down into the pitch-black corridor, Miss Fearsome's office on my right, the map of the London Underground on my left. I looked up to the alarm sensor to see that the blue post-it note was still in place. I smiled with satisfaction.

But now I had to move fast. I rushed along the hallway and turned left. The second post-it note was also still fixed to its motion sensor. I turned the handle to our classroom, opened the door and stepped inside. I moved across the room to Pea and Pod's tank and was about to lift the lid off when I heard a sound that turned my heart to ice.

As I'd approached the snail tank, my knee had accidentally pressed against a switch. The growl of a motor then started up. I'd unwittingly turned on the class fan, causing a blast of cold air to whip through the classroom. I immediately reached down to turn it off… but it was too late.

The cold wind had shot to the furthest reaches of the room and out the corner of my eye, I saw a blue post-it note flapping. After a quick struggle, it peeled away from the alarm sensor and then gently fell to the floor like an autumn leaf. My jaw fell to the floor like a heavy sack of spuds.

I froze for a moment in the silence, not daring to move, trying to control my breathing.

Nothing happened. The alarm didn't go off. And then I started to wonder if the post-it note had somehow deactivated it by covering it up for too long.

I decided to take a chance. Slowly, I moved my arm back to the snail tank and started lifting the lid. I reached inside to pick up Pod when I was shook out of my skin by the wailing sound of the alarm.

My heart leapt into my mouth. I picked up Pod with trembling hands before realising I'd overlooked something. I hadn't brought anything to carry the snails in!

I darted around the classroom, looking for something appropriate. As my breathing got faster, the howl of the alarm made my head feel like it was going to explode.

The first thing I found was a small pot, but it was full of pencil sharpenings and I didn't think the snails would like that. Then I saw it. The perfect thing. Next to our class plant stood a little metal watering can. It was pink and had a picture of a smiling lettuce on the side. Pea and Pod loved lettuce, so I knew that this must be a sign from God or Buddha or someone. Inside, the metal watering can was damp. This was also a good sign. Giant African Land Snails love moist conditions.

With my ears almost deaf from the alarm noise, I rushed over to the tank and grabbed the two snails. I placed them carefully into the watering can and legged it out of the classroom. I ran back down the corridor, leapt onto the table and out through the broken window.

As I landed on the ground, the alarm was suddenly silenced. I felt like I'd gone deaf. But then I spotted something scary. A car was now parked in the car park, Mrs Gillespie's car!

I ran around school towards the field, hoping to make my escape through the hole I'd dug. But then a beam of bright torch light flooded across the school field. Mrs Gillespie was inspecting the place. I wouldn't make it across the field without being spotted. I may have been wearing the Dora mask but Mrs Gillespie would be able to catch me up, especially as I tried to squeeze through the small hole.

I turned and ran, back towards the front of school. Mrs Gillespie had locked the gates after she'd come in, so I couldn't escape. Instead, I decided to hide. I skidded beneath the school minibus, pulling the little watering can with me.

I regretted wearing my yellow hoodie.

Why hadn't I picked a darker colour like blue or black?

If Mrs Gillespie looked under here, I'd be easy to spot.

Then, just when I thought things couldn't get any worse, I saw blue flashing lights approaching the school.

CHAPTER FIFTEEN: THE TRUTH

Watching from the shadows beneath the minibus, I saw Mum's friend, PC Jade Jackson, pull up in her police car, closely followed by our headteacher, Miss Fearsome.

They looked at the smashed window and searched the school. I never had chance to escape because – along with Mrs Gillespie – someone was always hanging around near the bus.

I felt doomed, destined to be carted off to prison like some of history's most famous criminals; Al Capone (the notorious American gangster), Bruce Reynolds (the mastermind behind The Great Train Robbery), Sideshow Bob (the nefarious hater of Bart Simpson). I'd soon be thought of as one the world's worst criminals; Jack the Ripper (the mysterious murderer), Billy the Kid (the infamous gunslinger), Will-i-am (crimes against music).

As the drizzle gradually eased off, the speed of my heart never slowed. Under the Dora mask, my breathing was heavy, my face super sweaty. I couldn't see any way out of this sickening situation.

After a while, PC Jade and Miss Fearsome came and stood near to where I was hiding. Jade had a pen and a notepad that she occasionally scribbled in.

"So, is there anything missing at all?" she asked our headteacher.

Miss Fearsome spoke in her gruff, smoker's growl.

"Everything seems to be in place. The computer room hasn't been broken into. All the safes are intact. And I've checked inside them. There's no money missing." Miss Fearsome paused for a moment and then shook her head. "There's just one thing. It's very strange. The snails from Class Five have gone."

Jade looked up from her notes. "Snails?"

"African Land Snails," said Miss Fearsome. "They're class pets."

"But why would someone take them? Are they valuable?"

"Not really. We got them cheap from Letchkov's."

Jade scribbled another note. "So why would anyone steal snails?" she asked.

Miss Fearsome reached into her coat pocket and then handed Jade a piece of paper.

"I found this letter outside my office," she said. "It claims that one of our teachers, Mrs Skarratt, is going to eat the snails. Very odd."

Jade frowned. "Eat them? So... do you think this Mrs Skarratt broke in to steal them?"

Miss Fearsome shook her head. "No. Why would she do that? If she wanted to take them home to eat, she could easily just pop them in her bag at the end of the day. But I did a walk around school before I left. The snails were still in there at six o'clock."

Miss Fearsome thought for a moment before speaking again.

"No, I think the person that sent this letter is the one who broke in. You know, to save the snails or something like that. They wrote their name on the letter but crossed it out. I think it says Jenny Grey but there's no Jenny Grey at our school."

PC Jade shone her torch on the letter. My stomach flipped.

"No," said Jade. "That doesn't say Jenny. It says Jerem–
Oh…"

Miss Fearsome took a step towards her. "*What* does it say?"

Jade turned off her torch and folded up the note. She attached
the torch to her belt and put the paper in her pocket.

"What does it say?!" Miss Fearsome repeated anxiously.

"Erm… maybe it *does* say Jenny Grey. I'll keep it as
evidence."

That was weird. Jade had almost read my name out loud but
changed her mind. She was covering up for me. But why?

"Perhaps we should question this Mrs Skarratt anyway," said
Jade. "Shall we do one last check of the premises?"

With that, the two women walked away. I sighed with relief…
but accidentally knocked over the watering can, which made a
metallic clang on the ground. Jade immediately turned, rushed
to the minibus and shone her bright torch into my eyes.

"Is there someone under there?"

I heard Miss Fearsome's voice rasp through the air, but
couldn't see her. I was blinded by the police torch. I felt like I

was going to wet myself with fear. My heart was all over the place like an out-of-control daddy longlegs.

After moving the torch away, Jade stared into my eyes for a hard few seconds. She couldn't see my face as it was hidden behind the Dora mask. She moved closer to the bus, crouched down and then whispered, "Is that you, Jeremy?"

I nodded. I could feel my jaw shaking. I wanted to cry.

Jade then stood up, turned away from the bus and spoke to Miss Fearsome.

"No," she said. "It's just a cat."

Miss Fearsome sighed. "Damn. I thought we'd got them. Never mind. I'm going to look at the fence, see if there's any damage." She then stormed off, away from us.

Once Miss Fearsome was out of sight, Jade turned back to the bus and crouched down again.

"I'm going to open the gate," she said softly. "Get out of here as soon as it's safe."

I thought my ears were playing tricks. She obviously knew about the damage I'd done to the school window. Why was she helping me?

She wandered over to the school gate, opened it and then disappeared to the opposite side of the premises, leaving me alone in silence for the first time since the alarm had sounded. I took a deep breath, grabbed the watering can and ran. I sprinted like a turbo-boosted cheetah until I was safely back at home.

*

I woke early on Saturday morning. I'd hardly slept at all. In the bathroom mirror I saw dark rings around my eyes that reminded me of a panda. A very tired panda.

Downstairs I found some lettuce in the fridge and shoved it into the watering can for Pea and Pod. As long as I had them, they'd never eat cornmeal again.

I sat at the kitchen table in my brown Chewbacca onesie and waited for Mum to come down.

"Morning Jeremy," she said, before pouring me a bowl of Coco Pops. She splashed on some milk and put the bowl in front of me. "Where's that pink watering can come from? Take it off the table please."

I grabbed the snails' temporary home and placed it on the floor.

"What time is Dad coming?" I asked.

Mum clicked the kettle on. "About nine o'clock."

I looked up at the clock. It was only five past eight. I tried to eat some Coco Pops to pass the time but didn't get very far. I had zero appetite. Instead, I just watched the milk turn chocolatey brown.

Mum busied herself with tidying and then switched on the washing machine. Just after half eight, she had a phone call. The bit of conversation I heard made my heart gallop.

"Broke into the school?" said Mum down the phone. "Smashed a window? Really? But they didn't take anything? Probably just teenagers with nothing better to do. Their parents should be ashamed, bringing them up like little thugs."

Yes, I thought. *Perhaps their parents should be ashamed.*

I heard Dad's car pull up at 08:54 (according to my trusty Casio).

"Jeremy!" said Mum when she saw me still sitting at the kitchen table. "Your dad's here. Go and get dressed."

As Mum ran off upstairs, I noticed that she'd made a particular effort to look pretty. She had makeup and lipstick on. She'd straightened her hair. And the scent of her most expensive perfume wafted through the kitchen as she went past.

I stayed at the kitchen table in my onesie and heard the sound of Dad beeping his horn. Mum came back into the kitchen.

"Jeremy! What are you doing?"

"Tell Dad to come in," I said. "I'm not moving until he does."

"I don't think you have time for this. He's taking you to Legoland today. You need to set off."

Typical, I thought. *I don't even like Lego.*

"Just tell him to come in," I said.

Mum sighed angrily. "Is this some sort of game, Jeremy?"

I shook my head. "Monopoly is a game. This is my life. Tell Dad to come in."

Mum squinted her eyes at me, as if trying to read my thoughts. Then, after Dad beeped again, she huffed and left the room. As I waited for them to come back, I became nervous. My heart raced at a billion beats per minute.

After a minute or so, Mum and Dad entered the kitchen. Mum looked embarrassed. Dad looked seriously annoyed, his face still covered in stubble.

"What's this all about?" he said. "Come on, little man. We're going to Legoland. We need to get going."

I had no intention of going to Legoland.

"Mum, Dad. Can you please sit down?"

My parents looked at each other with irritated expressions before deciding to do as I'd asked. I then picked up the pink watering can and placed it on the table.

"I'm pretty sure that I know what's been going on," I said. "A while back, my goldfish Fanny died. At first, I was a quite sad but didn't realise how badly her death would affect our family life."

"I didn't know you had a goldfish," said Dad.

"Well, you wouldn't know anything about our family, would you!" snapped Mum. "You were too busy with *her*."

This little exchange stopped me in my tracks. Dad didn't know I had a goldfish? But surely the pet was the thing that held our family together, wasn't it? If not, then my whole theory would fall to pieces. And who was *her*?

I carried on. "Because, as I learned from a tea towel, no family is complete without a pet. And looking after animals fills your heart with kindness and love."

Dad spoke to Mum. "What the hell is he going on about?"

"I don't know," she replied.

I carried on. "When Fanny died, you both lost some of the love and kindness in your hearts and before you knew it, our family was no longer complete. So, I now have something that will bring us all back together."

I reached inside the watering can and grabbed one of the snails. I pulled it out and placed it on the table in front of me. Then picked out the other one.

Dad looked revolted. "What in God's name are they?"

"Giant African Land Snails," I said. "Our new pets."

Dad looked at them like they were dog muck. "Insects?"

"They're not insects," I said. "They're gastropods."

"They're not living here," said Mum.

"We have to care for them," I said, "to help fill our hearts with love. Then you two will be happy again and can be proper parents that live together."

Dad shook his head and looked at Mum. "What's all this rubbish about filling our hearts up? Did you put him up to this? You think I'm going to move back in, just because he's got some snails?"

Mum scowled at Dad. "I knew nothing about this. I didn't even know he had these horrid things. And believe me, you are never moving back in here!"

"I saw it on a tea towel," I whimpered. I could hear the pain in my own voice.

Dad scowled at me. "Tea towel?" He turned to Mum. "What's wrong with him? Does he need to see a therapist or something?"

Mum smacked her hand against the table. "Yes! He probably does after all the psychological damage you've caused him!"

I couldn't believe it. My plan wasn't working. Their hearts were empty of love. They went on arguing for a few more minutes, screaming and shouting about me as if I wasn't even there.

I just stared out of the window. The drizzle had started again. Big tears of rain ran down the window pane. It felt like the sky was crying just for me.

As I stroked one of the snails' shells, real tears started forming at the corners of my eyes. I was about to tell my parents to shut up when Mum suddenly stopped talking. I looked up and saw that her eyes were wide, staring towards the kitchen door.

I turned around to see what she was looking at... and I couldn't believe my eyes.

"Is everything okay?" said Jade, standing at the kitchen doorway (not in her uniform).

Now I was in serious trouble. I pulled the watering can in front of the snails so she couldn't see them. But it was probably too late. The stolen goods had been sat there on the table when she came in.

Mum stood up. A red rage had taken over her face.

"What is *she* doing here?"

I thought this was a weird way to greet one of your friends.

I decided it was time to tell the truth.

"I think I can explain," I said.

Mum looked at me and then glared at Dad.

"Oh," she said. "Jeremy can explain, can he? I guess you've told him all about your new girlfriend then?"

"No," snapped Dad. "Actually, I was going to wait until –"

"New girlfriend?" I said. Then, I looked over at Jade.

"GET HER OUT OF MY HOUSE!" Mum's scream could probably have been heard in Mongolia.

And suddenly, everything made sense.

Mum and Dad splitting up.

PC Jade Jackson telling me not to be too hard on my dad.

Auntie Carol calling Dad a rat.

Dad saying that he'd be living with someone else.

PC Jade Jackson letting me off with two serious crimes.

Mum yelling at Jade.

Everything made sense now. Mum hadn't kicked him out at all. Dad had left her for another woman. PC Jade Jackson.

I felt sick. I couldn't believe I'd been so stupid. I'd blamed Mum. I'd told her that I hated her. I'd called her a stupid otter.

Dad stood up and moved towards the kitchen door.

"Come on, Jeremy," he said. "We need to go. The queue at Legoland will be massive if we're late."

I didn't move. I just sat there in my Chewbacca onesie. Thinking about how my life had fallen apart. And it was all because of Dad, the man who hadn't even known I had a pet fish.

"Jeremy!" he barked, standing by the door.

"Get lost, Dad," I said. "You're nothing but a waster. That's what you called my friend, Michael. But that's what *you* are. At least Michael knew I had a goldfish. At least Michael knows I don't like playing football. At least Michael knows I hate Lego. You don't know anything about me. You've ruined my life and I'm not coming to Legoland with you. You're worse than Henry the Eighth! You... you... you stupid otter!"

Dad rolled his eyes. "Whatever, Jeremy." He looked at Mum. "He needs to see a therapist."

Mum shook her head. "There's nothing wrong with my son. Now, get out of this house."

CHAPTER SIXTEEN: WHAT FRIENDS ARE FOR

Mum was meant to be working on that Saturday but she rang in sick and we spent the entire day cuddling on the sofa. We watched all of the Toy Story movies and I cried at them all. So did Mum.

We didn't talk about Dad at all. There was nothing really to say. And it would have only upset us both.

I felt like my plan had been a complete disaster but then Mum said she'd get a tank for the snails and I realised something. Maybe my plan had started to work. Love and kindness was already growing in her heart.

"They're kinda cute," she said as we fed them a few chunks of cucumber. "They're very gross but cute in their own way. If you like them, I'll let you keep them."

At those words, a little part of my broken heart began to heal. Still, I knew there were many cracks to fix. Dad and his new girlfriend had made sure of that.

On Sunday morning, Mum took me into town. We parked in Poundland car park, where a dishevelled bloke was having a wee against a lamppost. Mum nipped in to buy some shampoo, bubble bath, deodorant and a pack of razors.

"Why do you need razors?" I asked. "Do you have to shave your beard?"

"No," Mum answered. "They're for my armpits. Women don't have beards."

"Mrs Skarratt does."

After Mum bought the things from Poundland, we headed across the market place and when I saw the direction we were heading in, my heart sank.

"Where are we going?" I asked, despite already knowing the answer.

"Mr Letchkov's shop," Mum said. "You want a tank for the snails, don't you?"

I nodded but I knew that I couldn't go in there. If Letchkov saw me, he'd tell Mum about the crocodile eggs and try to fleece her out of another thirty quid.

"I think I'll stay outside," I said, as we approached. "Think I'd rather stay in the fresh air."

Mum frowned at me. "How will I know which tank to get?"

I shrugged. "How will *I* know what to get? Just ask Mr Letchkov."

Mum sighed, shook her head and then went in, the bell tinkling above her head as the door opened. I moved away from the shop, just in case the old Bulgarian came outside.

Town was pretty dead on a Sunday morning. I was standing alone in the middle of the very uncrowded market place, watching a one-legged pigeon hopping about, when I saw someone coming towards me. A woman I'd known for a long time.

The one-legged pigeon fluttered off with a manky chip in its mouth just as Michael's mum, Ama, got near to me. She looked anxious and I thought she was going to shout at me.

"Jeremy! Hello! I nid to spik to you pliz." Ama spoke with a strong West African accent and often shortened words. She said 'pliz' instead of 'please', and 'nid' rather than 'need'.

"Hello Ama," I said.

"Jeremy. You nid to mek friends with Michael. He is so upset."

"I don't know what you mean," I lied.

"He sez you fell out. You called him a liar and then he hit you. But he has bin so depressed since then. I know he meks things up but I think you should see thiz."

She handed me a pile of papers. They were letters, all written by Michael to his dad... the dad he'd never seen.

I read the first one. Michael's spelling wasn't great.

Deer Dad,

Hope your haveing a good week. I'm still saving munny to come to Ghana. Carn't wate to see you one day.

I've had a really bizzy time with Jeremy laytely.

He entered me into a karate competishon in Japan, so we asked NASA if we cud borrow one of they're rockits. They said only if we tested some rockits for them.

I didn't want to but Jeremy said it would be easy.

He's loads more braver than me. Anyway, wen we tested the first rockit, it crashed into the desert.

We had to eat cockroaches for a hole week.

Evenchually, this bloke came with some camels.

He said he wud let us have one if I kissed one of the camel's feet. So I did. The bloke and his friends laffed at me but Jeremy said it didn't matter as long as we had the camel. And he was *right. Jeremy is the most cleverist person I know.*

After we got out the desert, I had to nick a motorbike and then we drove to Japan and I won the karate competishon... all thanks to my best friend Jeremy.

Anyway, my munny pot is nearly full of 20p coyns now so I will soon be able to fly over to Ghana. Is it a big place? Will you be hard to find?

I will rite to you again next week.

Love you loads Dad

Love from Michael x x x x x x

Once I'd read the letter, I looked at it for a moment longer and then up at Ama. Her big brown eyes were watching me intently.

"What is this?" I asked.

"Michael writes thiz letters all the time. He wants to impress his dad so he meks up thiz crezzy stories. All his stories are about adventures with you. He thinks you are the best person in the world. This is why you think he's a liar. He just wants to impress his dad."

I thought about this for a moment. Maybe Michael didn't tell me his mad stories to show off. Maybe he just mixed up the real world with his fantasy world… the world he'd invented to impress his dad.

"But where is his dad?" I asked.

Ama shook her head, staring into the distance at a faraway memory.

"Michael's dad is a bad man. I pray to God that he will never see his dad."

I suddenly felt very silly and small. Sure, I'd had a bad time lately. My parents were splitting up and I hated it. But at least I still *had* my dad (even though – as I'd discovered – he was actually an idiot). Michael had never even known his dad and – if Ama had anything to do with it – he never would. His mum had brought him here when he was just a baby. She'd had no friends and Michael had no other family.

His only way of contacting his dad was through these letters of crazy imaginary adventures he has with me. And what had I done? I'd called him a fake, a phony, a fraud. I'd told him that all my troubles were his fault. I'd called him a waster and said that I shouldn't be hanging around with him.

Very painfully and very suddenly I felt like the worst person in the world.

*

Later that afternoon, I found Michael throwing stones at Harkington Mill. I approached him with a white flag (well, a white pair of pants tied to a stick) to show him that I didn't want to fight. When he looked at me, his face was filled with confusion and anger.

"What do you want?" he said, holding a rock rather too menacingly for my liking.

I stopped about four metres away from him. That was my estimate anyway. Estimating is like clever guessing. Miss Hope says that you should always estimate your answers in maths before you work them out. Then you'll know if your answer is close or not.

"I want to say sorry," I said. I could already hear the tears in my voice. "Sorry for being such a horrible pig. The things I said to you were out of order. You were just trying to be there for me. That's what friends are for, to be there for you when you're down."

I could see that Michael's bottom lip had started to tremble and I guessed that he was about to cry (or was I estimating?). I took a couple of steps closer to him, now about two metres away (definitely estimating).

"Look," I said. "I know that you make things up, but that's just part of you. You're my best friend in the entire solar system, so I don't even care. In fact, you're my best friend in the whole of Britain."

Michael laughed, his eyes wet with tears. "The solar system is bigger than Britain."

I moved right next to him and punched him lightly on the arm.

"You're a pretty good fighter," I said. "You smacked my nose well hard."

Michael nodded. "Well, I did win that karate competition in Japan."

"Yeah, I read all about that."

Michael's eyes widened. "What do you mean?"

"Your Mum showed me one of the letters you wrote to your dad."

Michael put his hands over his face. "No! Why did she show you those?"

I put my arm around him. "I thought it was pretty cool, mate. Me and you off on our adventures. I liked it. And it's a good way of talking to your dad, even though he's not here."

Michael moved his hands away from his face and smiled.

"I guess it is," he said.

"Maybe that's what I need," I said. "A way of dealing with stuff. Maybe we could write our adventures together."

Michael laughed. "Nah. I don't think we can make up stories together. My letters are kind-of personal."

"Okay." I nodded. "Listen, I might be in a bit of trouble. I broke into school and stole the class snails because Mrs Skarratt is planning to eat them. I smashed the school window while I was wearing a Dora the Explorer mask but I think the police know it was me."

Michael looked at me with confused eyes, his mouth slowly opening wider than a whale's. "What did I just say?" he said. "We can't make stories up together."

I shook my head. "No. This actually happened. I think I'm in trouble."

I explained about the letter I'd left outside Miss Fearsome's door and the way that PC Jade Jackson (the ugly cow) had let me escape. Michael said that no matter what happened, he'd be there for me... because that's what friends are for.

CHAPTER SEVENTEEN: SERIOUS TROUBLE

When we got to school on Monday, Mrs Skarratt was in a particularly vile mood. Her nostrils were flared like a furious bull and her eyes were filled with menace. She growled at Alfie Brown because his quiff was annoying her and she screamed at Leah Ford for breathing too noisily.

"I have asthma," Leah whimpered, trying very hard not to cry.

Mrs Skarratt gritted her teeth. "Well, suffer in silence. You sound like a hippo!"

We were given the brain-achingly boring task of copying the definitions of words from the dictionary. In silence. Sitting up perfectly straight.

I had a pretty good idea why she was being such a horror… because the snails had gone.

At ten o'clock, a message came for me to go immediately to the headteacher's office. A wave of panic rolled through my guts as I walked down the corridor that I'd become so familiar with. It felt much colder than usual because the window I'd smashed had been replaced with a blue plastic sheet, which made a flapping sound in the breeze.

I approached the office, passing the map of the London Underground, and then stopped outside. I could hear two voices talking inside. I recognised them both. I felt sick and took a moment to calm my breathing before knocking on Miss Fearsome's door.

The talking inside immediately stopped and then Miss Fearsome spoke in her gruff voice.

"Come in."

I took a deep breath and then turned the handle. Inside I saw Miss Fearsome sitting behind her wooden desk and, on a chair next to her, PC Jade Jackson in full uniform. Jade's face contained a strange mixture of worry, embarrassment and anger. She pouted her thick, ugly lips as usual.

The room smelled like old-fashioned perfume and mints. There was a photo of a lake on the wall and a poster of the human body attached to a cupboard door.

"Sit down, Jeremy," said Miss Fearsome, before barking out a deep, smoker's cough.

There were two free chairs. One next to Jade and one on the other side of the room.

I didn't sit next to Jade.

"Jeremy," said Miss Fearsome, "why do you think you're here?"

I pretended to think for a moment.

"Is it because I only got three out of twenty on Mrs Skarratt's spelling test?"

I noticed Jade roll her eyes.

Miss Fearsome just stared at me blankly from behind her brown-tinted glasses.

"No," she said. "I think you know why you're here."

I could feel my face burning red.

Miss Fearsome laid out the letter I'd written onto the desk and pushed it towards me. I gulped with guilt.

"Now," she went on. "The person who wrote this letter left it outside my office on Friday afternoon. They wrote their name but crossed it out. I thought it said 'Jenny Grey' from 'Year 5'. So, I checked the names of the Year 5 children but there isn't a Jenny Grey in that class."

Miss Fearsome pulled the letter away from me and looked at it. All the time, Jade was watching me. Miss Fearsome carried on talking.

"The person who sent this letter was very, very, very worried about those poor snails in your class, Jeremy. So, I decided to ring Miss Hope, who is now Mrs Bunyan because she got married last week. I asked her if there were any children in her class who were particularly fond of her snails. Do you know how many names she gave me?"

I felt a lump building in my throat. I shook my head.

Miss Fearsome looked at me over the top of her tinted specs.

"She gave me just one name. And then it made perfect sense because 'Jeremy Green' looks quite similar to 'Jenny Grey', don't you think?"

My breathing became tight as I sat there, fear churning in my stomach.

Miss Fearsome looked at the computer screen on her desk, she clicked a couple of times with her mouse before turning the screen around to me. What I saw was a still image from a CCTV camera. A small boy, wearing a yellow hoodie and a

Dora the Explorer mask, was about to throw a rock at the school window.

Miss Fearsome went on talking. "On Friday night, somebody smashed our window, broke into school and stole Mrs Bunyan's snails. It was recorded on our cameras but the person had cleverly covered their face. Fortunately, I recognised that yellow hoodie."

Miss Fearsome opened one of the drawers in her desk. She pulled out a piece of paper and placed it in front of me.

"Remember your school trip to Gulliver's theme park last year?" she said.

I looked down at the paper. It was a printed photo of three boys standing next to a life-sized plastic velociraptor. One of the boys was wearing a yellow hoodie.

That boy – of course – was me.

This was serious trouble.

After showing me the photo, the first thing Miss Fearsome did was ring my mum and ask her to come in. She already knew that my parents had split up (I bet big-mouth Jade had told her) so she rang my dad straight after but he didn't answer. She left him a voicemail.

My cheeks were soaked with tears and, when I eventually asked a question, I could barely get my words out.

"Am... am I... going to prison?"

Miss Fearsome and Jade both smiled in the same way, as if they felt sorry for me.

"You're extremely lucky," said Miss Fearsome. "We have insurance to cover the damages, so we aren't going to press charges. If we did, your parents would have to pay for a new window, which would be rather expensive. And you could even go to juvenile prison."

I felt lucky... but then guilty and ashamed. Mum would be mortified at the thought of me going to juvenile prison.

"You'll be serving your sentence here instead," Miss Fearsome went on. "You will have detention every lunchtime for two months and will be asked to do jobs around school, like cleaning, gardening or whatever else is needed."

After that, PC Jade left, telling me to stay out of trouble. Mum arrived about fifteen minutes later. Miss Fearsome explained what had happened.

Then I saw one of the most heart-wrenching things I've ever witnessed.

Mum cried for about half an hour.

No. She didn't just cry. She wailed, she moaned, she blubbered. She sobbed and sobbed right in front of me. Tears poured from her red raw eyes. She completely broke down in Miss Fearsome's office. She couldn't even look at me.

I felt yet another deep crack cut through my heart. And this was when I learned a big lesson.

My actions – my stupid, hot-headed actions – would always have an effect on other people. No matter how big or how small, everything I did would impact on something or someone. And my reckless behaviour on Friday night had completely shattered my mum's soul.

Really, I should have realised how foolish acts can impact on others. My dad had been so self-absorbed that he'd ruined the lives of the two people who loved him most.

I never wanted to make Mum cry again. Ever, ever, ever again.

*

After Miss Fearsome showed Mum out, I felt completely drained, as if I had nothing else to give. No more tears, no more energy. I felt like an empty school uniform, sitting in a chair with nothing inside.

When Miss Fearsome returned to her office, I noticed that her manner had changed slightly. Her eyes didn't seem as cold, her facial expression not quite as stony. Her croaky voice sounded smoother.

"You have to understand that this terrible act can't go unpunished," she said firmly. "My parents split up when I was a teenager so I know what you're going through."

I couldn't imagine Miss Fearsome as a teenager. I knew that all grown-ups were children once but I just assumed Miss Fearsome had emerged from the sea after a dark storm, looking exactly like she did today.

"I wanted to smash things and breaks things," she went on. "But you can't. People can't just turn into wild animals just because something upsetting has happened in their lives."

Then her voice softened and she said something that took me by surprise.

"I do have to ask you a question though, Jeremy."

She opened her drawer again and pulled out my letter once more.

"What's all this nonsense about Mrs Skarratt? Cleaning her boots? Kissing her feet? Eating the snails? These are quite bizarre accusations."

I swallowed and tried to speak. My voice came out in a small whimper.

"It's all true."

Miss Fearsome looked at me over the top of her tinted glasses.

"So, you actually broke into school to save two insects?"

"They're not insects," I said. "They're gastropods." I'd have thought a headteacher would've known the difference.

Miss Fearsome shook her head. "But why would Mrs Skarratt do *any* of these things?"

I thought for a moment. It was pretty hard to actually remember.

"Erm… She made me clean her boots because I laughed at something Michael Nkrumah said. And she made me kiss her feet because of the Year 5 curriculum."

Miss Fearsome arched an eyebrow. "What do you mean?"

"We had to work out the areas of different circles, so I told her that it isn't on the Year 5 curriculum."

"You're right. It's not. That's secondary school stuff."

"So then she made me kiss her feet. And they smelled like Stilton cheese."

Miss Fearsome paused for a moment before gazing casually at the letter again.

"Can you prove any of it?" she asked. "Would anyone else testify to any of this?"

A pang of dread hit me. Everyone was terrified of Mrs Skarratt. They wouldn't want to cross her. And most people had been avoiding me like a rabid dog since I'd kissed the old hag's talons. I doubted anyone would back me up.

Then I remembered someone who would stand by me no matter what.

"Michael Nkrumah," I said.

Miss Fearsome rolled her eyes. "Michael Nkrumah couldn't keep his story straight if he used a ruler. That boy has an extremely vivid imagination. He once told me that he'd had pilot lessons when he went to Africa."

"That's probably something he wrote in a letter." I sighed. "He's never even been to Africa, apart from when he was a baby."

"Precisely," said Miss Fearsome. "Isn't there anyone more reliable that would speak to me?"

I didn't think anybody else would grass on Mrs Skarratt, so I shook my head.

"And what about the snails?" Miss Fearsome asked. "Why do you think she was going to eat them?"

I explained about the book, *Catalan Cuisine.* About the cornmeal and the purging process.

Miss Fearsome wasn't convinced. She said that my emotions had obviously been running high and I was probably jumping to wacky conclusions. Then she told me something that tightened my breathing again.

My mum was going to return Pea and Pod to school tomorrow.

I couldn't let this happen! After everything I'd been through – after everything *Mum* had been through – we couldn't just hand the snails back to Mrs Skarratt.

I had to stop her!

CHAPTER EIGHTEEN: PARROT FEVER

I pleaded with Mum not to send the snails back to school but it was no good.

"Do you think I'm going to listen to you after what you've done, Jeremy?"

She sent me to my room and grounded me for two months.

I didn't sleep very well that night.

After realising how awful a person I'd been recently, I found my cousin Floyd at playtime the next day (yes, I was still allowed out at playtimes, just not lunchtimes). I apologised for every time I'd been horrid to him. He forgave me.

I told him and Michael that Mum had brought Pea and Pod back to school and that Mrs Skarratt would definitely eat them. Definitely! I explained that I'd told Miss Fearsome about Mrs

Skarratt's plans and that she'd made me kiss her feet but Miss Fearsome hadn't believed me.

"I just need to accept defeat," I said. "I've caused enough damage to everyone."

"You can't just give up," said Michael. "Pea and Pod need to be saved. They may be slimy and disgusting but we can't let Mrs Skarratt eat them."

"Yeah," agreed Floyd.

"When my mum was in Ghana," Michael began.

I stopped him right there. "This isn't the right time for one of your tall stories, Michael."

Michael shook his head. "No. Hear me out. This one is true. When my mum was a kid in Ghana, her school had a class parrot. Everyone loved it. It even learned to say some words."

"What," said Floyd. "Like 'Who's a pretty boy?'"

"No," said Michael. "The parrot didn't speak English. Anyway, after a while, all of the children in her class started getting sick. Like really bad flu. The doctors told all the children they had something called Parrot Fever. Their parents did lots of things to try and stop the illness. Medicines, tablets, washing their bodies in milk. They tried praying, they tried voodoo, they tried eating nothing but pineapples for a week. But still the children became sick with this Parrot Fever."

"So, what language do they speak in Ghana?" asked Floyd.

Michael ignored him. "Eventually, with almost everyone in the school poorly, one sensible person finally had a good idea. He told them to stop the problem at the source and get rid of the parrot."

"And then what happened?" asked Floyd.

"Well, they got rid of the parrot and everyone got better." Michael held up his hands. "Sometimes it just takes a different way of thinking."

Floyd screwed up his chubby face. "What's that got to do with the snails? If you release them, they'll just get eaten by an eagle or something."

Floyd may not have understood the message behind Michael's story but I got it loud and clear. The gears in my brain were turning faster than ever. An idea was beginning to form in my head.

Stop the problem at the source.

All of a sudden, I knew how to save the snails… and this time, I wouldn't need to break any laws. As we made our way back to class, I quickly told Michael and Floyd about my master plan.

This could well be our last chance to save Pea and Pod.

*

Mrs Skarratt was still trying to teach us about the areas of circles.

She'd been droning on for an eternity when I eventually spotted Floyd waddle down the corridor, past our classroom. My Casio watch told me the time was 11:03. Floyd nodded as our eyes met through the window. I nodded back. The game was in play.

"So," shrieked Mrs Skarratt from the front of the class, "which one of you nitwits can tell me how to get *pi* on your calculator?"

The day before, Mrs Skarratt had explained that 'pi' was a number you used to work out the area of a circle. It was a ginormous decimal that started with 3.14159… but that's as much as I could remember.

Having seen Floyd trundle past our class already, I immediately put my hand up to answer.

"Green," the old hag snapped. "Do you know how to get pi on your calculator?"

I nodded. "Go to the *Pie Minister*. It's this pie shop in town. They do allsorts. Chicken and Mushroom, Steak and Kidney, Meat and Potato. I bet you could get some pie on your calculator there."

I heard a few people snigger, but Mrs Skarratt's face turned a dangerous shade of pink.

"Excuse me?!" she growled.

"Why?" I asked. "Did you fart?"

The hag's cheeks went from pink to purple. There was practically steam coming out of her ears.

"How dare you!" She spat these words out like venom. You could literally see the saliva forming at the corners of her mouth. She tried to wipe it away with the back of her filthy hand.

"Come here!" she barked, before starting to untie the laces of her boots.

I looked at Michael and grinned. The old goat had taken the bait.

There were a few gasps as Mrs Skarratt once again peeled away her yellow-stained grey socks. Her talon-like toenails were thicker than ever, as were the bristling black hairs on her toes. The massive wart still stood proudly on her right foot, like a saluting soldier.

The Stilton-like stench sent me dizzy for a moment as I knelt before her.

"You seem to have forgotten how to respect me," Mrs Skarratt hissed. "Now, bend down and kiss my feet. Remind yourself who's in charge in this room."

With the poisonous fungal foot fumes attacking my nostrils, I had an urge to be sick. Where was Floyd? If he didn't hurry up, all of this would be pointless and would just give everyone another reason to treat me like a leper.

"Come on!" Mrs Skarratt roared. "Get on with it!"

I saw her raise her hand and, for a second, I thought she was going to hit me. So, trying not to breathe through my nose, I slowly lowered my head towards her filthy feet.

Come on, Floyd. I thought. *Where are you?!*

My puckered lips languidly moved towards Mrs Skarratt's terrible trotters. I lowered my face, further and further, my mouth moving closer and closer… until… the classroom door burst open.

"MRS SKARRATT!!!"

Miss Frearson's fearsome voice was an almighty roar.

"WHAT ON EARTH IS GOING ON HERE!?"

She charged into the room and yanked me to my feet, moving in front of me as if to protect me from Mrs Skarratt.

"Well, I was.. I was just… checking my feet and then he came and kissed them. That boy, Green."

I heard Miss Fearsome growl. She actually growled like a hungry lion. Then her voice became scarily quiet.

"Mrs Skarratt. Collect your belongings and remove yourself from the premises immediately. You will never set foot in this school again and I will make it my personal mission to make sure that your teaching days are over!"

Mrs Skarratt looked around the room. She wanted to say something, to get her out of the hideous hole she'd dug for herself. But she knew there was no way out. Miss Fearsome had seen her, punishing me with her vile, twisted foot-kissing ritual.

We all watched as she shoved her things, including the *Catalan Cuisine* cookbook, into a bag. I moved in front of the snail tank, where Pea and Pod had been rehomed. Once Mrs Skarratt had packed her belongings away, she approached the tank.

"I don't think so," said Miss Fearsome, in her gruff voice. "Those snails belong to school."

Mrs Skarratt stopped in her tracks, her piggy eyes piercing into mine.

Miss Fearsome searched the faces in our class before pointing at Herbert Humphreys, the cleverest lad in our class.

"You," she said. "You're in charge until lunchtime. Teach them something about decimals." Then she turned to the dirty, snail-eating witch. "Right, out you go. These children deserve better than you and they don't ever want to see you around here again."

Defeated, Mrs Skarratt sighed, walked out of the room and left our lives forever.

CHAPTER NINETEEN: SNOT AND TEARS

At lunchtime, I was made to help out in the school kitchen, washing everyone else's dirty dishes. I went into the kitchen in an upbeat mood. Mrs Skarratt was gone and the snails were safe. A part of my life had finally improved. It felt like a long time since that had happened.

But as I stood there, feeling the soapy water get greasier with each plate I washed, my mind started to recall the events of the last two weeks.

My dad had turned out to be one of the most horrid people on the planet. He'd run off with a pouting policewoman and left Mum to fend for herself. I'd ruined my own reputation, especially in Mum's eyes, by smashing the school window. And now I was stuck doing dirty jobs for Miss Fearsome during my lunch break… a punishment I thoroughly deserved.

I felt tears roll down my cheeks and my whole body started to shake as I broke into a full-on blubbering howl. My tears dripped into the dishwater and my sniffles were so loud that I didn't notice the other person come into the kitchen behind me.

"Jeremy?"

With just that one word, Miss Hope's voice was as smooth and sweet as syrup.

I turned around quickly, trying to wipe the snot and tears from my face.

"Miss Hope? What are you doing here?"

Her bright smile made the dull greyness of the school kitchen feel instantly warmer. Her belly was still as round as a beach ball. She hadn't had her baby yet.

"My name is Mrs Bunyan now, Jeremy. Why are you crying?"

At first, I just said I was upset about my parents and told her about Dad running off with PC Jade Jackson. If it had been anyone else, I probably would've kept my mouth shut. But Miss Hope (yes, I'm still calling her that) made me feel warm and safe, so I just told her.

I started to cry again and Miss Hope pulled me in for a hug. Then she looked away for a moment, searching her mind for a distant memory.

"When I was nineteen," she said eventually, "I had a boyfriend, Dale. He was the most gorgeous man I'd ever seen. I thought we were going to get married, have children, everything. But then he split up with me. Completely out of the blue. At first, I was devastated. I cried and cried until I couldn't cry any more. But, step-by-step, day-by-day, I slowly got over him. And since then, I've had a totally wonderful life. I met Luke not long after and now we're married and about to start our own family."

"What happened to the old boyfriend, Dale?" I asked.

Miss Hope shrugged. "I see him around town, every so often. He's an idiot who still hasn't grown up. And that's what I'm trying to say. If I'd still been with him, I'd be miserable. I wouldn't be anywhere near as happy as I am now."

We were interrupted for a moment by a dinner lady, bringing in a load more dirty dishes for me to clean. Miss Hope said hello and then waited for her to leave again. Once the dinner lady was gone, Miss Hope continued.

"I know it's difficult to understand but your Mum and Dad may not have been happy for a long time. That sometimes happens with grown-ups… they grow up, then grow apart. If your Mum and Dad stayed together, they might be miserable for the rest of their lives."

I'd never thought about it like that before. It was a daunting thought, knowing that Mum and Dad might need to separate in order to enjoy their lives again. It was a heck of a lot to take in.

"It'll take time," Miss Hope continued. "But I bet your mum will be happy again soon. Step-by-step, day-by-day, you and her will start to feel brighter again. Until, eventually, you will feel something like yourselves once more. And long after these dark times are behind you, you'll realise that this pain you're feeling right now will have made you both stronger. You'll appreciate your happiness more than ever. And when you do feel happy again, you'll feel happier than you ever thought possible."

It was hard to accept but Miss Hope was probably right. After that, I told her about the snails and Mrs Skarratt and the break in. Everything. I don't know why. It all just came spilling out.

Miss Hope listened, her face changing from shock to horror to sadness. And before I knew it, I was crying again.

"But it was all for nothing," I sobbed. "Because the snails didn't save my parents marriage. It was a stupid idea in the first place. And now everyone hates me for smashing those windows."

Miss Hope smiled sadly.

"The thing is," she said, "life is tough. It's complicated. You had an interesting idea that you thought would help. It might have worked but you can't force people to think or feel or behave in a certain way. Sometimes you just have to accept the things that are out of your control and deal with them the best you can. Like the weather."

"The weather?" I said.

"You can't control the weather," said Miss Hope. "But you *can* deal with it. When it's cold and rainy, you wear a coat. When's it's hot, you wear a cap and sun cream. You can't change everything, Jeremy. But sometimes, you *can* make a difference. And that's what you did."

I frowned for a second.

"Why? What difference did I make?"

Miss Hope smiled. "You saved Pea and Pod."

I laughed and then shook my head. "No. I don't think many people would accept that smashing a school window to save two slimy snails was a noble act. I'm not exactly Joan of Arc, am I?"

"Maybe not," she said. "But I know you're not a troublesome child, Jeremy. Just tell me that you won't do anything like that again."

I shook my head. "No way. I've learned my lesson. I never want to upset my mum like that again. I just want to help her get through all of this now, to deal with it. Like the weather. Because, in her world, there's a horrible blizzard at the moment and she needs some of my warmest hugs."

Miss Hope smiled. "Good on you, Jeremy. Well, I'm going to sort those snails out before I leave. They must be bored out of their minds with all that cornmeal in their tank."

With that, she went over to the fridges on the opposite side of the kitchen. She opened one and pulled out a whole iceberg lettuce. She closed the fridge door, winked at me and then rushed out, leaving me with a pile of greasy plates, gravy dripping into the now-cold water that was no longer soapy.

CHAPTER TWENTY: OUR NEW LIFE

Being grounded was boring but I knew I deserved it. Plus, it would keep me out of any more trouble.

After tea I went up to my room and started drawing. At first, I was just doodling but my doodle quickly turned into a snail shell. It looked cool so I did another one. After a while, I'd filled two whole pieces of paper with drawings of snails.

Then I decided to make a comic. The snails were creatures from another planet. They came to Earth to eat as much lettuce as they could because lettuce gave them super-powers on their own planet, Gloopiter, that would protect them from their attackers.

I drew the evil villain, Mrs Skarratt. She was also an alien, but from a different place – The Planet of the Frozen Hearts. Her planet wanted to attack the snails' planet and eat all of the creatures who lived there. So she came to Earth to stop the snails from getting the magical lettuce.

Luckily for the snails, there were two amazing humans on Earth who would stop the evil Mrs Skarratt. Their names were Jeremy Jaguar and his sidekick, Michael Mandrill. I loved mandrills. They were my favourite type of monkey. I mean, they have a red and blue face! What more could you want?

When I drew me and Michael in the comic, we both had sharp teeth. My face was covered with black spots. Michael's was red and blue. We looked like cool super heroes. I reckoned Michael would love my comic.

I'd just finished colouring the final picture of our adventure when Mum came into my room. Her eyes were red so I knew she'd been crying.

"You don't have to stay up here all night," she said. She smiled at me but the sadness behind her eyes was so deep that it made me upset. "Do you want to come downstairs and watch a film?"

We went down and snuggled on the sofa with duvets and cushions galore.

"I'll put your favourite on," she said. "Toy Story."

I *did* love Toy Story but I was a bit grown up for it now. Still, I didn't say anything because I knew Mum liked watching it with me.

Halfway through the film, I heard her sobbing. In fact, I felt her body jerking as she cried. I knew that she wasn't crying at the film because it wasn't a sad bit, just Buzz Lightyear being stupid. She said it was her hay fever but I knew this wasn't true.

She was obviously thinking about Dad.

Thinking of what Miss Hope said, I tried to cheer her up.

"You know what, Mum. Dad is just a rain cloud. You just have to deal with him until the sun shines again."

Mum stopped crying and looked at me.

"What are you on about?" she said. "Have you been writing poetry?"

"No," I said. "I've been making a comic."

She shook her head. "Well, what's all this rain cloud business."

I tried to remember Miss Hope's words.

"Dad is like winter. You can't control him and he's depressing. So just wait until it's summer again. Then we'll be happy."

Mum laughed. "I have no idea what you're talking about but it's cute." She sighed as she thought for a moment. "You do know that you'll have to start going to your dad's new house soon."

I had thought about it and I knew that I'd have to do it. I didn't want to at all but I'd already accepted it. Dad's new life had begun. I just wish it hadn't hurt Mum so much.

"And what are we going to do about that snail tank now there aren't any snails in it? It's full of soil but I think we could our money back if we give it a good clean."

I wasn't so sure. Mr Letchkov would probably find a reason to keep the money.

Still, once the film had finished, I went upstairs to fetch the tank and took it outside to clean. I was about to tip the soil out into the garden when I noticed something.

In amongst the dirt were a load of little yellow pebbles. The pebbles were tiny, about one tenth the size of a penny. Normally, it wouldn't have been strange to see pebbles mixed in with soil but there was something different about these pebbles… and they definitely hadn't been there when we first put the soil into the tank for Pea and Pod.

I picked one up. It was extremely light and delicate. And that was when I realised. They weren't pebbles at all. They were eggs. Tiny snail eggs. About thirty of them in total.

I rushed back into the house to show Mum. She started crying again (shock) but these were tears of joy. She was happy. She actually wanted the pet snails.

And then I realised something else. My mission hadn't been a total failure.

Looking after animals fills your heart with kindness and love.

We finally had pets in the house. Mum was smiling and our new life was about to begin. Our new life… with thirty tiny new lives.

IF YOU ENJOYED THIS BOOK
(OR ANY OF DANIEL HENSHAW'S OTHER BOOKS)

PLEASE LEAVE A KIND
AMAZON REVIEW

NOTES FROM THE AUTHOR

I would like to say a massive thanks to everyone who has ever supported my writing, ever since those early days when I was making up short stories about talking clothes pegs (honestly). As any author will tell you, all feedback is useful, particularly when you're starting out, so I'd like to start by saying a big thanks to Roz, Beccy and the all of the White Peak Writers, past and present, for all their help over the past few years. Joining your wonderful group really helped me to start believing in myself.

Secondly, I want to show my gratitude to a special lady named Dorothy Naughton, who became an important, helpful and ultimately supportive figure as I dived into the scary world of writing books longer than 25,000 words. Thank you Dorothy.

Next, I think I need to say how grateful I am to the children and staff at Annesley Primary School. You are a constant and continuing source of inspiration.

Thanks to my family for everything you've ever done. You've always been there without hesitation and you'll never know how grateful I am for that. Thanks to my 'editor' Debbie for her eagle-eyed comma watch. And, of course, big love goes to my Fern. I couldn't have done this without you.

A massive shout goes out to this book's awesome illustrator, Jimmy Rogers, whose cover design has taken this project to a whole new level.

And last but certainly not least, I'm sending warm hugs out to all of the Jeremy Greens and all of the Michael Nkrumahs out there, just trying to make sense of this weird world in which we live. Stay out of trouble kids!

Daniel Henshaw

Daniel Henshaw is the author of '**The Great Snail Robbery**', '**The Curious Case of the Missing Orangutan**', '**Jeremy's Shorts**' and '**Glenkilly**', all starring Jeremy Green. Daniel is a qualified **primary school teacher** and holds a **degree in English Studies**.

In 2016 one of Daniel's unpublished stories was shortlisted in the '**Best Novel for Children**' category at the **Wells Festival of Literature**. A recording of his short story, *'Grandad's Ghost'*, was aired on **BBC Radio** in 2020. He lives in **Derbyshire** with his girlfriend and two cats, Morse and Thursday.

Follow Daniel on Twitter: **@AuthorHenshaw**

Or **Facebook.com/JeremySnails**

DANIEL HENSHAW'S BRAND NEW BOOK

GLENKILLY
IS OUT NOW!

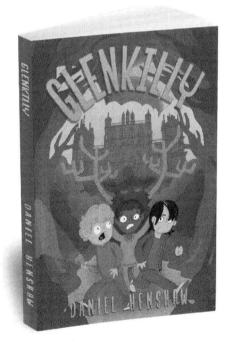

TURN THE PAGE TO READ THE FIRST 3 CHAPTERS...

CHAPTER ONE:
UNLUCKY FOR SOME

I had a feeling we were in Scotland. The sky had darkened, the fields were full of hairy Highland cattle and I'd seen a big sign that said *'Welcome to Scotland'*.

We were here for camping, which sounded scary enough – with the breeze and the bats and the bagpipes – but my nervousness increased with each mile as I watched the terrifying scenery through the coach window. The Scottish countryside was full of danger. Armies of dark pine trees stood in great clumps, as if they were hiding some chilling secret, and – in the far distance – huge, deadly mountains were half-hidden by swirling clouds. The safety of towns and people had quickly become a distant memory.

There was a stinky, stale atmosphere on the coach – all bad breath and boredom – and for hours on end, I'd been squished between the window and my best friend, Michael. He'd taken the aisle seat, claiming to have a *'window allergy'*, which sounded far-fetched, even for him.

"Aren't you worried?" I asked, despite knowing that Michael never worried.

He arched a casual eyebrow. "About what?"

"This trip. We're camping in the middle-of-nowhere."

"You don't need to worry, Jeremy. Just relax."

"*Relax?* How can I relax? Have you not seen the size of those cows' horns? How are we meant to defend ourselves? We're only ten."

"They're just cows, Jeremy."

I shook my head. "And what about today's date?"

Michael shrugged, secretly scoffing the bag of *Mini Cheddars* that our teacher, Mr Hopton, had specifically told him not to open. "October?" he eventually said.

"October the *thirteenth*," I added.

"So what?"

"The *thirteenth*. Thirteen is an unlucky number."

Michael looked at me blankly. "Is it?"

"Yes! My mum says that bad things always happen on Friday the thirteenth."

"But, Jeremy, it's Monday."

"And she says that the skyscrapers in New York don't have a thirteenth floor because it's such a bad omen. *Thirteen. Unlucky for some.* That's what Mum always says."

I sighed, my breath fogging the glass as I scanned for danger outside. The bumpy country roads had narrowed now and dark trees towered over us, draping the coach in a blanket of shadows.

"I've never been camping before," I admitted. "What if I can't do any of the activities?"

Michael laughed. Finishing his *Mini Cheddars,* he screwed up the packet before wiping his fingers on his tracky bottoms. "Come on, mate. You'll be fine. You're good at *some* things. Like that picture of a wasp you drew. That was… *alright*."

"Thanks mate."

I smiled, though I wasn't quite sure how useful a drawing of a wasp would be on a school camping trip. Still, I bent my arm and pointed my elbow. Michael did the same and we gently tapped elbows. It was our special thing. We'd always wanted a secret handshake but couldn't do any of the complicated ones we'd seen on YouTube. So we had the Elbow-Bump instead.

Our coach then slowed right down and our driver flicked on the indicator as the roadside trees parted to reveal an electric gate in the middle of a tall iron fence. It didn't look like the entrance to a campsite, more like a prison, or worse, a school.

The gate suddenly jolted, before slowly… very, very slowly… sliding open, as though unsure about letting us in. Once inside, a long, winding drive led up a small hill towards a gloomy building on the horizon, silhouetted black against the grey October sky.

Although the place was named Glenkilly Castle, the building barely resembled a *castle* at all. There was no moat or drawbridge, no turrets or cannons. It was more like a stately manor house with gleaming windows running along the walls, like a hundred square eyes, and ghastly gargoyles glaring down from the roof.

Stepping off the stifling coach, the cool Scottish air felt heavenly against my grubby skin. The autumn sky was grey and sunless and it already felt too cold for camping.

There were twenty of us on the trip altogether, along with our teachers, Mr Hopton and Mrs Dodd, and we gathered by the side of the coach as the driver passed us our belongings. I thought *my* bag was over-packed but Michael's enormous red rucksack was so heavy he almost toppled over when he put it on his back. Every time he moved, it rattled like a tin of marbles and I couldn't begin to imagine what was in it.

We then headed towards the castle, everyone chatting merrily as our feet crunched across the gravel car park. And that's when we spotted the badger.

Now, I'd seen some pretty disturbing things during my first ten years on Earth – men with hairy backs, steaming cow pats, Auntie Carol's lasagne – but this was the worst. The badger lay at the edge of the car park, stiff as a board, its eyes glazed over. Weird bald patches ran across its back, where a gang of squabbling magpies were greedily pecking at the poor thing's flesh. And, yuckiest of all, blood spattered from its mouth as though it had swallowed a whole bottle of ketchup before throwing up.

"You think it's dead?" said Michael.

"Looks pretty dead to me."

No one else had noticed it.

"Should we tell Mr Hopton?" I asked.

Michael shook his head. "Nah. He'll only panic."

In all honesty, glaring down at the poor animal, having its guts nibbled by magpies, *I* was starting to panic. What sort of place was this, where they leave dead animals lying around for children to see?

"I used to have a pet badger," said Michael.

I didn't respond. Michael had a habit of bending the truth. He once told me he'd seen a goat driving a Ford Fiesta through Asda car park. How its hooves were supposed to have reached the pedals, I really don't know.

"What do you think killed it?" I asked as we moved away, crossing the car park towards a paved path at the front of the castle.

"Probably a wolf," said Michael.

My nerves tightened. "Do they have wolves in Scotland?"

Michael nodded. "I saw one on the way up here."

"You never mentioned it. And you didn't even sit near the window."

He didn't answer.

As we approached the castle's big wooden doors, I noticed something rather odd. Other than the excited chit-chat of our classmates, everything else here seemed quiet... too quiet, like in a doctor's waiting room, or a maths test. I couldn't see any other school groups. No children racing around, no teachers being forced onto the zip-line… nobody at all. Weird.

As we climbed the stone steps in front of the wooden doors, the coach hissed behind us before rumbling into action. I glanced around to see it heading back towards the electric gate, its noisy engine startling the greedy magpies. They scattered in an explosion of black and white feathers, flying off to perch on a nearby telephone line.

I counted them silently.

Thirteen magpies.

Thirteen.

Unlucky for some.

CHAPTER TWO: JUST JEREMY

The castle had a musty smell – of wood and leather – and it reminded me of *The Horse and Jockey,* where I sometimes went for a carvery with Mum.

We were ushered into a warm sitting room filled with old leather sofas, varnished coffee tables and a stained tartan carpet. A cosy log fire hissed and crackled inside a grand stone fireplace, which had a coat of arms impressively carved into it and a huge antique clock on the mantelpiece.

Portraits of miserable old men lined the wood-panelled walls and a rusty suit of armour stood motionless in one corner like a frozen robot. A massive stag's head hung above the door and I wondered how long ago the animal had died. Five years ago? Fifty? Five hundred? Maybe they'd have the badger on the wall next week.

"Hi, guys! Welcome to Glenkilly Castle."

The voice came from a tall man standing by the fireplace. He spoke with a Scottish accent so smooth he could have been an airline pilot. Although well into his forties, the man had a diamond stud in his ear, teeth bright enough to be seen from outer space and skin so orange he reminded me of… well, an orange.

"My name's Hamish, and this is Kat."

By his side, stood a youngish lady, with a trendy pair of spectacles framing her eyes. Like Hamish, she grinned an enormous grin, though her teeth were a more natural shade of white.

"Hi, everybody." Kat spoke in a high-pitched, pixie voice. Waves of orange hair curled down past her shoulders and a million orange freckles were scattered across her nose and cheeks. "We're your activity leaders here at Glenkilly," she said. "And we're looking forward to a fun, fantastic week with you all."

Both Kat and Hamish wore green uniforms with the words *GLENKILLY STAFF* stitched into their jackets. They gave a quick speech about moving safely around the grounds and mentioned some of the exciting/slightly terrifying activities

Special Preview!

we'd be doing this week: canoeing, zip-lining, go-karting. They also warned us not to drink the tap water, because they were having problems with the plumbing, so each of us was given a bottle of Highland mineral water and a shortbread biscuit.

Once they'd finished talking, I shuffled over to a huge bay window with Michael. Looking out, I saw fields running for miles around – as though the castle were floating on a sea of green – and further away from the building stood the black forest, like a shadowy perimeter fence, surrounding the grounds on all sides.

As I nibbled a biscuit, I was about to ask Michael which activities he was looking forward to when something peculiar caught my eye. Poking its head above the woodland, I spotted a tall metal structure, a bit like a giant tower of scaffolding. Hundreds of pine trees huddled tightly around it, like bodyguards protecting an important leader.

"What's that?" I asked, pointing out of the window.

Michael peered past me. "Looks like the Eiffel Tower."

I raised an eyebrow but said nothing. Something about the tower made me uneasy. What was it? Some sort of extreme climbing cage?

Thanks to the creepy castle and the dead badger and now this strange tower, I felt jittery. Michael wouldn't get it. He never worried about anything. Usually I'd go to Mum for reassurance but she was a billion-trillion miles away, back home. Across the room, I spotted Kat standing alone. She seemed nice, so I headed towards her, squeezing past my classmates through the crowded room while Michael stayed by the window.

"Howdy," I said as an introduction. I'm not sure why. The moment the word left my mouth, it sounded ridiculous and I silently vowed to never, ever say 'howdy' again for the rest of my life.

Kat looked down at me and smiled. I noticed a small hoop pierced into her nose and a rainbow of cotton bracelets wrapped around her wrist. *Hippie Bracelets.* That's what Dad would've called them.

"Hello there," Kat answered, her voice pillow soft. She lowered her head towards me, and I caught the sweet scent of her perfume, like fresh flowers. "What can I do for you?"

"Hi, um…" I suddenly felt nervous for some reason. "My name's Jeremy. Jeremy Green. But people call me… just Jeremy."

"Hello, Just Jeremy."

"No, it's just… Jeremy."

"Okay, Just… Jeremy. What can I do for you?"

I frowned, unsure what to make of her. "Um… well, could you tell me what that tower is in the middle of the forest?"

Her eyes shifted around the room. "The tower? That's, erm… nothing to worry about. Did you get a biscuit? And a bottle of water?"

I raised my empty bottle, noting that she hadn't actually answered my question. "I also saw a badger. Near the car park. Just as we were coming in."

Kat's face brightened. "Oh, that's great. There's plenty of wonderful wildlife for you guys to see around here. You're quite lucky to see a badger though. They're actually nocturnal."

"It was dead."

"Oh."

"Its skin had come off and magpies were eating it."

Kat's eyes widened in horror and the colour drained from her face. "Oh, erm…" She glanced at Hamish – but he was busy telling Mr Hopton about the cereals available at breakfast.

"Right," said Kat, turning back to me. She nervously tucked a strand of orange hair behind her ear. "Well. There's no need to panic."

"I'm not."

"It's just the circle of life, you know. Sadly, animals die all the time. It may have been hit by a car or perhaps it was just old. I'm so sorry. You weren't supposed to see that."

Kat smiled – though her anxious eyes never changed.

You weren't supposed to see that.

What did that mean? Her worried expression told me that she wasn't being honest. But what exactly was she hiding?

Kat smiled again, before turning back to Hamish and taking him by the arm. She delicately moved him away from Mr Hopton.

Not wanting to miss out, I stepped closer.

"That weird kid over there says he saw a dead badger," Kat murmured. "With *skin* missing."

Weird kid? What did she mean?

Hamish sighed, scratching the stubble on his chin. "They weren't supposed to see any of that. Go and shift it."

Kat nodded before darting from the room.

Those words again.

They weren't supposed to see any of that.

Now my head was abuzz with questions. Why were they so bothered about a dead badger? Why did they not want us to see it? Why would a man in his forties wear a diamond stud in his ear?

Then my insides shrivelled – because, judging by the way that Hamish was glaring at me, I realised I'd just asked all of those questions… out loud!

Weird Kid.

Special Preview!

CHAPTER THREE: ROTTING RABBITS

"Jeremy Green! Pay attention!"

Our teacher, Mr Hopton, had a nasally voice like a strangled goat. It snapped me from a daydream as an icy wind whistled through the archery range and grey clouds hovered above. Having set up camp – shoving our bags into a tent and laying out our sleeping bags – we were now crowded around Hamish, the walking midlife-crisis.

"Whenever you're loading your bow, guys," the activity leader was saying, "keep the arrow pointing away from your friends, preferably towards the floor or the target."

"Safety is extremely important!" Mr Hopton bleated.

"Make sure the nock fits onto the bow, guys, just beneath the nocking point." He placed the arrow onto the bow.

I hadn't been listening so I had no idea what a 'nock' was – or a 'nocking point'.

"You'll know when it's in the right place, guys, because you'll hear it click."

Something clicked.

"Pull the string all the way back to your cheek. And then release." He let go of the string and the arrow flashed to the target, hitting the yellow circle in the middle. Everyone clapped.

When it was my turn, I followed Hamish's advice. I tried to pull the string right back and keep my arms steady and all the rest of it, but my first shot failed to even reach the target. Connor McCafferty sniggered as my arrow nestled pathetically into the grass. I turned around to scowl but Connor – his black fringe almost hiding his eyes – was whispering something to the other boys before pointing at me. A chorus of cackles followed, causing my face to glow.

Connor thought he was the *Bad Boy* of the class. With a black stud in each ear, he wrote rude words on tables, stuck chewing gum on teachers' cardigans, and walked on the grass when there were clear signs that said, '*Do Not Walk on the Grass.*' His black hair hung below his ears, often covering half of his face. He seemed to think this gave him an air of mystery, like a rock star or a James Bond villain. But really, he just looked like one of those dogs that can't see because of its overgrown fringe.

By the time I'd finished my six shots, not a single arrow had reached the target. I tried to blame the wind but nobody listened.

"Nice one, *Jellyfish*," Connor sneered.

More laughter from the crowd.

He'd been calling me *'Jellyfish'* ever since we learned about them in class.

A jellyfish doesn't have a brain.
A jellyfish doesn't have a heart.
Some jellyfish are invisible to the human eye.

He's only jealous, Mum always said, which was pretty hard to believe as I'd just watched him hit a tiny yellow archery target with six arrows. *Just ignore him,* were Mum's other words of wisdom, which was also pretty hard to do when everyone in class laughed along with him.

Then I remembered Dad's words. *Man up.*

I felt my nostrils flare.

Clenching my fists, I stepped towards Connor, ready to take him down.

But it was no use.

Without flinching, Connor straightened, towering over me, his dead, shark-like, brown eyes glaring from behind his black fringe.

Like a true wimp – a person who was afraid of mud and moths and men in kilts – I instinctively cowered, skulking in fear like the Hunchback of Notre Dame.

Man up?

More like 'man down'.

Defeated, I retook my spot at the back of the crowd… as far from Connor as possible.

Jellyfish have no backbone.

I huffed. Archery was stupid anyway. It wasn't like anyone needed to shoot arrows these days, was it?

No longer interested in this pointless activity, I gazed around at the grounds. Glenkilly Castle stood such a distance from the archery range, it looked like a tiny bungalow from here, surrounded by acres of green fields, all penned in by the forest.

I was about to turn back to the archery when my eye caught on an odd shape in the grass nearby; some sort of animal. Stepping away from the archery range, I moved towards the mysterious object. The creature lay perfectly still, about the size of a small cat, with light brown and greyish fur.

I crept closer.

Again, it didn't move.

Was it sleeping? Injured, perhaps?

I took one more step… before realising it was…

Urgh! A dead rabbit!

My mind flashed to the badger.

Two dead animals in such a short space of time.

I'd seen a dead pigeon in town once but this was far worse. Like the badger, most of the rabbit's fur had fallen out. I could even see some of its bones, with tiny insects crawling all over the remains.

A cheer from the archery range disturbed my observations. But as I was turning back to my classmates, I noticed a second animal about five metres away. Curious, I wandered over to the small clump of brown fur. Sure enough, it was another lifeless rabbit – a second scrawny body, chunks of hair missing in a similar way with hundreds of little bugs invading the poor rabbit's flesh.

Peering across the grass, I noticed a third rabbit, missing fur, just the same.

Then a fourth.

And a fifth.

I felt like Hansel, or Gretel (whichever one was the boy), but instead of a breadcrumb trail, I had a trail of rotting rabbits to find my way back.

But why so many dead bunnies?

I stepped over to a sixth carcass, and before I knew it, I'd trekked across an entire field and was standing at the edge of the black woods.

Special Preview!

Staring into the tangle of trees and bushes and branches and leaves, I couldn't help but notice how dark and eerie it looked inside the forest. Even in the middle of the afternoon, the woodland was draped in sinister black shadows, making it hard to see anything clearly.

I glanced down at the sixth rabbit, missing so much hair it was almost bald. What could possibly have happened? The rabbits didn't look like they'd been attacked. But it was strange how they all looked so similar. All skinny, all hairless, all… dead. And their trail had led me to this spot at the edge of the gloomy woods, where an overly-sweet scent hung in the air. It smelled like the flowery jasmine air-freshener my mum used, though I couldn't see any flowers in the woods.

I was turning to leave when…

Crack!

What was that? A snapping twig? Was someone there?

Staring into the dark forest, my eyes fixed on a set of branches jutting out from a tree. They looked sharp and dangerous and, for a moment, I thought they could be antlers.

I tried to focus. With all the shadows, I couldn't tell whether my eyes were playing tricks on me… but something

looked to be moving, just ever so slightly. Breathing, maybe?
My heart hammered so hard, I could practically hear it.

And then I froze, barely daring to breathe myself, as I
realised what I was seeing.

There, about ten metres ahead, half-hidden behind the trunk
of a wide tree, someone – or some*thing* – was staring right at
me… with bright red eyes.

Daniel Henshaw

Special Preview!

HAVE YOU READ DANIEL HENSHAW'S OTHER BOOKS YET?

FOLLOW DANIEL HENSHAW

 ON TWITTER: @AUTHORHENSHAW

 OR AT WWW.FACEBOOK.COM/JEREMYSNAILS

DANIEL HENSHAW
AUTHOR DAY & KS2 MYSTERY WRITING WORKSHOPS

Daniel also visits schools! Most recently he's been to…

London: Gordon Primary; **Liverpool**: Springwood Heath Primary;

Cheshire: Adswood Primary; **Northamptonshire**: Beanfield Primary, Oakley

Vale Primary; **Nottinghamshire**: Annesley Primary, Morven Park, Dalestorth

Primary, Robert Mellors Primary, Wainwright Primary, Samuel Barlow Primary,

Hawthorne Primary, Mount Primary; Brinsley Primary, Kirkby Woodhouse;

Derbyshire: Tansley Primary, Loscoe Primary, Horsley Woodhouse Primary,

Coppice Primary, Wirksworth Junior, Ashbourne Hilltop, Hady Primary

> **"Daniel's whole school assembly was exciting and funny. He did**
>
> **exactly what we had hoped, capturing the children's imagination**
>
> **and really inspiring them for a day of writing mystery stories."**
>
> Robert Mellors Primary School, Arnold, Nottingham

If you're interested in this opportunity, email: **mrdhenshaw@gmail.com**

for details.

Printed in Poland
by Amazon Fulfillment
Poland Sp. z o.o., Wrocław

64381571R00139